Reign

Brutal Kings
Book 3

Via Mari

Chapter 1

Serena

I wake to the Vegas sun shining brightly into the room, completely sated after a night of lovemaking, but filled with a dread that will not go away. I squint, stretching to check my phone for the time. It's early, but Giovanni is already gone. Early meetings are a reality for him and his high-powered friends. It is what I counted on, and the only reason I allowed myself to sleep in. I am a coward, but there is simply no way that I can do this face to face. He will be as devastated as me, but it is the only way to ensure my family's safety.

I slip out of bed and get dressed for the day, eyeing myself critically in the mirror. The mango-colored capris and cream-colored button blouse with wedge sandals reflect a woman who is outwardly confident, but that's a far cry from reality. My heart is pounding heavily in my chest while my blood races a million miles a minute through my veins. I inhale deeply, trying to calm myself, taking in large quantities of air. I've made my decision, and it is for the best, but that doesn't stop the anxiety or the ache in my heart as I gather my things, place them in a large shoulder bag, and walk out of the penthouse, away from the man that I will love forever.

I nod to the bodyguards who enter the elevator with me as I make my way to the main floor of The Larussio Resort and Casino.

While these men are big and intimidating to those around us, they are anything but to me, usually friendly and cheerful. I have a feeling they won't be too friendly shortly.

"Gio is still in a meeting, but we have instructions to escort you to the café on site. It's one of the few places in the casino that's already finished and open for business, outside of the actual gaming rooms. Gio had it and one of the restaurants finished for all of the workers, along with your penthouse and our security area," Nick says as the others leave us to take up their stations within viewing distance.

I nod and inhale a deep breath before I drop the news. "He's thoughtful like that, but I won't be having breakfast here. I'm going to Italy and need to be on a plane very quickly."

He starts to say something, but I cut him off with a show of my hand. "I know Giovanni won't be pleased, but he will be even more displeased if I ditch my security team with everything happening," I say, sincerely remorseful that I'm putting Nick in this position.

His eyes go wide. "He's not going to just be displeased; your boyfriend is going to hit the ever-loving roof! You should have seen him last night when he thought you were taken by Dominic Mancini's men. No disrespect, Serena, but you're *really* going to put him through that again?" he asks.

I turn because his words give me pause. I know exactly how I would feel if Giovanni were in danger, but this cannot be helped. The only way to save my family from the hell that will eventually rain down on them is to remove myself from the equation. Giovanni knows this. He tried to push me away for the very same reason, to keep me safe, but I ruined that little effort.

If I am not with the future Don of Italy, then my family will be safe from his enemies. I thought I was strong enough and I could go head to head with them. I can, because I have been trained, I am prepared, but only if they come after me and not my family, not my beloved nonna.

I inhale deeply, as if the breath alone will give me the strength I so desperately need to pull this off. "Don't think this is easy for me, Nick. I love Giovanni with all my heart, but I will not allow my nonna, brothers, and their families to be harmed because of my self-ishness. I thought somehow it would be okay, that Giovanni could fix this, but it will never go away if they want to see him broken." My voice cracks, but I refuse to let my tears fall in public. "I'm trying to do this with as little drama as possible. Please, just take me to the airport and get me to Italy. I'll take it from there."

Nick's eyes narrow at me, and he shakes his head. "You know I won't leave you, Serena. I'll take you where you need to go, but not making Gio aware is out of the question. I'll give you ten minutes, and only because you didn't try to slip out of my sight and were up front and honest. Ten minutes from now, I'm going to let Giovanni know that you're heading to the airport," Nick says, texting out a message before grasping my arm gently, intending to guide me outside into the fresh air.

"That is not long enough. It's no time at all! You know Giovanni will have one of your security friends come after me or stop me at the airport. Maybe I should have just ditched you," I huff at the burly security guard.

He laughs out loud. "They told me you were pretty mellow, no drama. Ha! A ten minute head start in this traffic is all you need, and that's all you're getting. The jet is being inspected as we speak, and the crew is preparing for the flight. You and I will be on that plane before Gio has time to get to the airport."

I stop walking and turn to him. "Wait one minute! You are not going with me past the airport. The entire point is to disappear, to get clear of Giovanni and all of his family. I can't do that if one of his security team is with me!"

His jaw sets firmly as he glares down at me. "You don't have a choice in the matter, Serena. I'm not about to lose my job because I let the future Don of Italy's woman put herself in danger. Sorry, but you're not going anywhere without my protection, and that's the end of this discussion," Nick says, taking my arm gently again.

I'm not going to win this argument, and I know it. He clearly has everything in motion, and I grudgingly respect it. "Fine," I huff, allowing him to guide me to the limo that pulls up curbside. He assists me into the back seat just as the mammoth man they call

Cole slides into the seat next to me, then Nick hops into the front seat and slams the door closed.

Nick turns to make sure I'm buckled, and I narrow my eyes at him. "Really? And how is Cole a part of this? Why is he here? What happened to giving me ten minutes?"

He shrugs unapologetically and grins at me. "We're your team, you need twenty-four hour coverage, and one man can't do it alone. Stop scowling at us like that, or I'll give Giovanni a text now instead of waiting another six minutes," Nick says, tapping his watch and chuckling under his breath as the driver veers out into the heavy Vegas traffic.

I glance around outside, half expecting Giovanni and the rest of his team to come barreling out of nowhere to stop me, but then relax. For some reason, I believe that Nick is honorable and will keep his word not to alert Giovanni right away. The airport isn't far away. The driver seems to know his way in and out of the morning traffic, and we're soon pulling onto the private tarmac of the Las Vegas airport. It takes us moments to get through security, and as soon as we're cleared, Nick and Cole guide me up the ramp and onto the sleek white Larussio Gulfstream.

Nick gestures for me to go ahead of him as we enter. "Make yourself comfortable. I just let Giovanni know that you're gone, and he may have a team coming after you. I asked the pilot to take off immediately," Nick says as the plane door closes and the engines roar to life.

I've been on aircraft like this thousands of times, working as a service attendant on some of the most luxurious private jets ever built, but the opulence of the Larussios is remarkable. I take a seat in one of the soft white leather recliners and try to swallow down my nerves as I watch out the window.

"This is the captain. We're about ready to take off. Buckle up, ladies and gentlemen," he says, and the aircraft begins to move, quickly gains speed, and begins barreling down the narrow concrete runway. It is only by sheer will and determination not to cry that the tears which have pooled, blurring my vision, do not fall.

We careen past the palm trees, cactus, and yellow desert life that are all waving in the breeze. The jet lifts into the air, climbing slowly, and then gathers speed, soaring into the whitest, puffiest clouds and clear blue sky that I have ever seen, while taking me farther and farther from the man I love.

Nick and Cole stay seated across from me, until I assure them that I'm fine alone and that once we level off I will be heading into the master bedroom to sleep for at least part of the flight between Vegas and Italy. I slide out of my shoes and settle my feet underneath me, watching as the clouds swirl around us, and pull a blanket around me to dispel the cold and emptiness inside. Nick and Cole head into the security room behind the main cabin, and I turn on my cell phone, bracing for the inevitable.

> I will find you! BTW- You have just earned a punishment spanking.

Chapter 2

Gio

This business meeting is one of the last needed to finalize The Larussio Resort and Casino in Vegas. It's the only reason I'm here and not in bed with my dark-haired beauty wrapped around me, with my cock deep in her heat. The scantily clad waitress dressed in a black and white ensemble prances around the conference room, placing orange juice in front of us, while a fully dressed waiter balances a heavily laden tray of breakfast plates.

As soon as everyone has been served, I start the presentation for the city's elite, letting the group know the progression of The Larussio. I don't go into much detail about last night's exclusive members-only grand opening because it's been splashed all over the local papers, which, along with every entertainment magazine that caters to the who's who around the globe, have been extremely positive. Instead, I share plans for finalization and elicit their feedback for a more public-focused grand opening in the near future for the city that never sleeps. Uncle Carlos, head of the New York crime family and the man responsible for The Larussio vision, has joined us today via teleconference and is all smiles this morning as he listens to what his daughter Katarina and I were able to achieve.

The men and women who run the city of Las Vegas are excited

about the opportunities the new and expansive resort provides in terms of employment, and especially the draw that it will have on privileged and monied members who will spend many of their dollars in the community. I can see wheels turning as the leaders contemplate not only the profits, but what being able to engage with global tycoons of this magnitude can provide in terms of monetary assistance with other endeavors to enhance their city in the future.

The well-dressed brunette at the end of the table has just broached the topic that was on my mind and that I would have engaged the group in had she not done so by the end of the meeting. *Always best to let them raise the idea themselves. Let them own it.* One of the best pieces of advice I ever received from Uncle Carlos, the man who was my mentor when I was a young entrepreneur trying to break free from the family mold.

The woman leads us into a discussion of private airstrips and tarmacs. The clientele we intend to bring in will not be flying commercial, and they certainly won't want their arrival announced at a public airport. Discretion on every level is expected, and the people around the room are well versed in the necessity for this. I let them banter different options around as they eat breakfast, amused and intrigued by some of their ideas, but glance down at my phone as it buzzes.

> Serena wants to go to Italy without telling you. Cole and I are with her. We will keep her safe.

I read and then reread the message, and my entire chest tightens with fear. Serena was unusually quiet last night. She was exposed to what being with someone like me really means, and believing her nonna had been taken by the enemy shook her to the core—the very reason I was unable to sleep, got up earlier than normal, and then listened to the damn recording our security team made of her attempted kidnapping last night. The threats to harm her nonna, the woman who practically raised her, would shake anyone, especially someone new to this ugly world where attempts on our lives happen daily, something that will never change, because the Larussio crime family has enemies everywhere.

I should have known it would cause her to contemplate continuing our relationship. The expense of her family, one that she cherishes deeply, is too steep a price to pay. I thought I could keep her safe—I *know* our security team can keep her safe—but hearing firsthand what someone would do to her nonna was clearly too much for her.

I send a message to Jay, the head of our security team, and my cousin Salvatore, asking them to meet me in my penthouse in fifteen minutes, before texting Nick to care for Serena until I give him further instructions.

I then message my spirited dark-haired beauty, letting her know that I will find her, adding that she has just earned a punishment spanking for her trouble. She had her chance. I tried valiantly to do the right thing to keep my enemies from learning about her, but whether she is with me or not, they now know what she means to me, and that alone means she is at the top of every single one of my enemies' lists.

The next ten minutes of the meeting I should be heavily invested in but don't give two fucks about right now passes in a blur. It's unlikely I'll recall in half an hour a single word anyone has said. All I can think about are the heads that are going to roll when I get Jay alone. I blame him and the entire security team for Serena being distraught enough to leave!

The meeting ends with the town's assurance to contribute to a new private airstrip and a helipad space where the resort's guests can land and avoid the Vegas traffic and paparazzi. I thank everyone for their time and contributions and am the first out of the conference room. I stalk my way toward the elevator that will lead me upstairs to the penthouse that was completed just one week ago for me to share with Serena, the woman who is now miles above us, completely unreachable, flying away from me instead of lying in my bed naked and needy and awaiting my return.

Two security members get into the elevator with me to head upstairs. Small talk is not something I'm interested in right now, and they seem to sense this, a survival instinct I'm sure, and they are smart not to say a goddamn word. The doors open into my penthouse living room, and Jay and Salvatore are already there, which doesn't give me one minute to contemplate what to say, or to cool down, which is not good for anyone.

I march directly to Jay, grabbing his lapels. "You and your shadow games. Serena is petrified for her nonna, and she left!" I say, barely controlling my rage.

He nods. "You're not going to like what I have to say, but please, just hear me out. She knows exactly what could happen to her or any of her family if she decides to stay with you. From a security standpoint, she needs to be fully aware of the dangers. You knew that. We talked about it, and you wanted me to make sure she fully understood. It was the only way to keep her safe last night, when things started to go down, and to make sure she was fully aware of the danger. The fact that she took her security detail with her this morning, and didn't run off alone, means that she fully comprehends the dangers. We need her to understand the full reality of what we're dealing with if we're going to protect her from Mancini."

I hear him talking, but I'm not even *near* fucking ready for a voice of reason. I try to contemplate what he's said, but that doesn't change the fact that she is gone. My dark-haired beauty is already heading back to Italy, flying far, far away from me. A choice of words, or any response at all, seems to elude me, but my anger does not dissipate; it only smolders just below the surface, ready to erupt into a full-blown volcano at any time.

Jay knows I'm as pissed as he's ever seen me, but he doesn't cower. Instead, he looks me right in the eye as he speaks. "Nick and Cole are good men. They're on the plane with Serena, and they won't let anything happen to her. As soon as we can clear Antonio and get him on a plane without drawing suspicion, he'll be on his way to Italy to join them. She's used to him protecting her and will feel more secure."

"Where? Where in Italy? Where are you taking her?" I finally manage to get out, while tightening my grip instead of loosening it from his lapels.

"Nick and Cole are taking her to your family home, Gio. She isn't safe anywhere else, as you and I both know. We haven't told her that yet, so Nick and Cole will need to have that conversation when they land. She wants to go to her brother's house. We'll try to get her to stay at your family home, but we can't hold her against her will when they arrive. It's not our way. If you read our contract, you'll see it spelled out to the letter."

"Fuck your contract! I wasn't asking you to keep her imprisoned. I just want her to be safe," I bellow, and as soon as I listen to the words and rewind everything that has happened in the last twelve hours, I realize Jay and the entire security team have done exactly what I would have wanted. She could have left without security, and he is right, she did take her protection because she saw the risks firsthand. I am just having an extremely difficult time reconciling the fact that after everything we've been through, she decided to leave, and that's on me, on the goddamn family that I am part of, and not on the security team who has done nothing but protect the two of us and our families.

I let go of Jay's shirt, taking in the steely eyes still fastened intently on my own. "I owe you an apology. I know you're trying to keep the entire family safe, and you're right, I wouldn't want Serena held against her will, but she's running scared, Jay, and that's on you and your team."

His eyes narrow, but he steadfastly holds his ground, which impresses me despite my mood. "She's scared because she should be, which is exactly why she didn't ditch her security team when she left. We've learned the hard way that we need to ensure the people we are safeguarding know exactly how vulnerable they are if not guarded. Chase and Brian will attest to this, Gio. You have my word that her safety is my and my teams utmost concern, even if our methods piss you off."

No one dares to speak to a Larussio in this manner, and Salvatore's entire body tenses, causing a chain reaction throughout the entire security team, each one on the ready for a sudden move, but I shake my head to keep Sal refrained. "I already know that you are committed, or you sure as hell wouldn't be standing here. Keep Serena and her family safe at all costs."

He takes my threat in stride. "She'll be completely safe until she hits Italy. Salvatore, we're going to need help navigating things with your great-uncle once she gets there. We'll need lifts to some of the security clearances that you and your uncle have set up. We're going to need our best men on the ground and inside the complex if everyone's going to come out of this alive," Jay says.

Sal nods, one curt gesture. "We can talk when we're home," Salvatore says, and he doesn't need to say a word. Nothing that would bring trouble to the family is going to be discussed until he is confident that we are in a place where no one can listen in on the conversation.

Chapter 3

Serena

The moment we're airborne, I climb into the luxurious master suite bed fully dressed and open my laptop to connect with Wi-Fi and begin the research that I need. If Antonio finds out that I took his password one day while he was in the bathroom, he'll probably never forgive me, but I need to know exactly what I am up against, not just what the family and security team wish to tell me.

Dominic Mancini was once a formidable enforcer for the Chicago Mafia, but he thought he could do better on his own. He marshaled some of the Chicago crew and slowly began pilfering money from the Chicago mob and dabbling in other illicit activities to gain an even greater foothold in the crime industry. According to records, Dominic was using Ty Channing, a well-known attorney, to launder money through the Torzial Consulting Firm.

The company name looks so familiar. I rack my brain trying to remember where I've seen it before, when I see the name of Katarina Meilers-Larussio-Prestian, Giovanni's cousin. She works for the Torzial Consulting Firm, and her boss and best friend is Jenny Torzial, the woman who was accused of murdering Ty Channing, her fiancé and the lawyer who worked for Dominic. Damn, what a small world!

Jenny was acquitted of all murder charges, but it was learned that unknown to her at the time, Ty was using her company and passwords to funnel Mafia money through her company. When the Chicago Mafia learned Mancini was skimming, they came after both Mancini and Jenny Torzial. Now it's all coming together!

I continue to read, skimming through pieces here and there, some I am already aware of, but I slow down when I get to the part about Giovanni. Mancini and his crew initially taking asylum with the Italian family rumored to have turned him out of their safe house, which is how he was caught by the authorities and now sits in one of the harshest prisons in the country. This is what Giovanni was referring to. He is the cause of Dominic being captured by the authorities! Damn. No wonder the man has a vendetta against him and anyone he cares about.

Dominic's network, at least those who haven't already been taken out, are apparently still alive and well. Every two days he has a phone call that he takes in the break room, and prison officials believe information is provided and instructed via code, but they haven't been able to break it to understand the instructions he sends out to his still loyal team on the outside.

My family and I have done nothing, but Giovanni's enemies want to hurt me to hurt him. They've certainly tried, but he hasn't let them get to me, and he still has an entire security team at his disposal to battle Mancini's loyal supporters on the outside, and that's clear from reading Antonio's notes, which gives me some peace of mind. I place my laptop on the nightstand, turn my phone off, and try to get a little sleep.

It's been hours in the air; a nap, a little bite to eat, watching mindless movies and a shower later. I finally turn my phone on and watch as the barrage of messages, eleven in total, appear on my screen. All from Giovanni, all indications of his displeasure and concern. I swallow through the pain of his messages, and the one that hurts the most is his disappointment in me not talking to him about my concerns. I don't blame him for the way he feels, but we both know I wouldn't have been strong enough to walk away if I had talked to him about it first. As much as I hate to admit it, he always knew the truth. He did everything in his power to send me away, knowing that we had to give each other up in order for my family to stay safe. I was the one who didn't fully realize how bad it could get, regardless of how forthright and candid he was.

When the plane lands, it's morning in Italy, incredibly early morning, which means that very few people are moving around and active, but Nick and Cole have made me a cup of coffee in one of the travel mugs onboard. I inhale the aroma, and before I even taste it I know it will be delicious. A perfect balance of espresso and hazelnut and cream. Absolutely divine!

"This smells amazing," I say.

Cole hands me a lid. "Bring it with you. We need to get going."

The men open the airplane door, and we are immediately surrounded by an entourage of intense and gorgeous looking security men, all with headsets affixed to their ears, keeping me surrounded as they lead me down the ramp and into an awaiting limo. They get me settled into the car and then split up into the vehicles that will both lead and follow our car.

The driver heads to the highway, and after a half hour or so the landscape becomes extremely familiar. This is not where I told them I wanted to go. I asked them to take me to my brother's so we could work on a plan to keep our family safe and come for Nonna when we knew it was okay, but that's not where we're heading, and I know exactly where they are taking me.

"You want me to trust you, to come to you when I have fears and need you to keep me safe, yet your allegiance is not to me. Time and time again you do Giovanni's bidding! I told you to take me to my brother's home! My family is not safe, and it's going to get worse and worse if they find out that I am at the Larussio estate. I will be a prisoner, nothing else!"

Nick and Cole both have the good grace to look chastised. "Look, Serena," Nick says, "we work for Giovanni and the family, but that doesn't mean we don't understand what you're going through. We want to make sure you get through it alive. We wouldn't be here otherwise. Giovanni's estate is the safest place for you to be right now. We were going to talk to you about it, but thought it might be better to do it once we arrived. We are in the process of moving your nonna too."

"Wait, why? No! She will absolutely hate it! You must know how badly she feels about the Larussios. She will *never* take to living under their roof. I can't subject her to that!"

Nick's eyes narrow at me. "Would you prefer to watch her be killed? Perhaps with a random missile dropped from a drone like they did with your grandfather's house? Maybe this time they won't miss. Or maybe they'll drop the missiles all around, enough to give us a chance to get her out of the house, but then just take her. We are good, Serena, make no mistake about that, but you and your family are not safe unless you are at Giovanni's estate, at least for a short while."

I shake my head. "No, this is not what I envisioned. I already called my brothers, and they had a plan to keep me safe until I could come for Nonna. This way, the enemies wouldn't know where I was or come for Nonna, because they would believe I left Giovanni. That was the whole point, to make them think that we're not together!"

"Serena, I hate to state the obvious, but it's far too late for that. They know that you are Giovanni's because you led them right to his estate. No matter what you do, that will never change. They also know where your nonna is. How do you think they followed you into town and out to Giovanni's? They have eyes everywhere. That's what we're dealing with and trying to sort out, but you have to trust us and give us time to do our job."

"I do trust you, but my brothers are expecting me. We have to figure out a plan to keep them and their families safe."

Cole's been quiet the entire time, just taking in our conversation, but he finally takes pity on Nick. "I'm sorry you have to go through this, Serena, but we're not going to let your family be taken. We know what we're doing, and we overheard the conversation that you had with your brothers. We're going to handle everything," he says.

He doesn't look even slightly fazed as my eyes go wide with shock. "You did not! Where is that goddamn wire? Tell me right now, Cole!" I demand.

His jaw tightens. "I can't do that, Serena. Suffice to say that we heard the conversation, and your brothers and their families are safe. They're going to meet you at the Larussio's estate. In fact, your nonna is being prepared for transport as we speak. We didn't want to move her until you were with her, so the troops on the ground will move her at my say so."

"At your say so? Do you have any idea what you've done? She will never forgive me, and she will hate Giovanni even more now. How on earth did you convince Great-Uncle to take my family in? They are not cleared in any way! What if they want nothing to do with the family and turn on them? What then? Did you think about that when you were making decisions for my life without asking me?"

Cole narrows his eyes at me. "Calm down, Serena, and one question at a time! Your brothers will not turn on anyone. It will be your job to ensure they don't have a reason for ill will toward the Larussio Family. They were already hiding their families, Serena. Giovanni wanted them safeguarded, and that's what we're doing."

"Giovanni wants it, and that's how I have to live. Alone, without him, in a huge villa, kept a prisoner from life!"

"It won't be forever, and remember, now you will have your nonna and your family. You won't be alone."

My phone buzzes with a message from Giovanni, and I huff at the fact his security team tells him absolutely everything!

> I will be home shortly after you land, and we will discuss this with you across my knee!

<h1 style="text-align:center">Chapter 4</h1>

<h2 style="text-align:center">Gio</h2>

If Serena thinks for one moment that I will allow her to hide out from Mancini's men in her brother's home, she is wrong, no matter how much her grandmother or brothers disagree. Great-Uncle has already secured clearance for her family, knowing full well when he did that it may come to this sometime in the near future. I wasn't prepared for her to leave, but perhaps it's for the best that she knows just how serious Mancini is, even if she doesn't yet see the need to stay at my family's estate. I glance down at the ding of an incoming message. My dark-haired beauty has a mind of her own, and I chuckle as I read her response.

> I am NOT a child! You had no right to bring me here!

Oh, on the contrary, I had every right, because she belongs to me to protect and safeguard, to love and cherish, and yes, even to paddle when she can't seem to get out of her own way. I smile broadly as the team walks me to the jet that will have me in Italy before my naughty little submissive knows it.

Are you ignoring me, Giovanni Larussio?

I can hardly contain my laughter as we board the jet, and the engines begin to roar. The security team gets the cabin closed up, and I settle in and send her a message.

Do not worry, tesoro. Things are under control at home.

Nonna will hate it; your great-uncle will be livid!

I glance up, and Salvatore is watching me. "Is everything ready for Serena and all of her family?" I ask, ignoring my cousin's smirk as continual dings of incoming messages hit my cell, letting us both know that my little sweetheart is far from finished with her tirade.

"I made arrangements for the guest houses while you were at your last meeting, so everything should be set when they arrive. All of Serena's nonna's medical equipment has been transported, but Serena is seriously pissed. The security team tells me she's fuming mad," Salvatore says.

I run my hand through my hair and smile at him. "So I heard. Thanks for taking care of everything. Any luck finding her brothers' wives? Where the hell did they stash them?" I ask.

"I think they believe this is some sort of setup to have their families come out in the open. Paranoid fuckers! I don't blame them for wanting to keep the women and children protected, but they'll be much safer at our estate than anywhere else."

"Yeah, have you heard how Great-Uncle's taking it all? I wish one of us were there to calm him. I wasn't too keen on him leaving directly after the grand opening or flying home without us, but now I'm glad that he did. At least he'll be there when Serena arrives."

"He's beside himself. I'm telling you, Giovanni, if you ever decide to break it off with Serena, he may disown you. He's become quite fond of her, wouldn't even start coffee or breakfast until she joined him each morning when she was staying at the estate. They seem to have formed a genuine bond. And my sources tell me he's been on the phone with both the housekeeping manager and head chef, giving them instructions for the guest houses and meals."

I smile widely because only a short time ago Great-Uncle was the very one warning me away from Serena and wouldn't even allow her to step foot in our penthouses without clearance. Funny how that woman has managed to worm her way into the heart of more than one Larussio. "I wouldn't consider breaking it off with Serena. I'm going to marry that woman, Salvatore," I say, flipping through pictures of her I have saved to my phone.

Salvatore chuckles. "I wondered how long it would be before you decided to pop the big question. She's a keeper, Giovanni. She thinks the sun rises and falls with you. Most of the women I meet want a lifetime of money and leisure. She is a feisty little thing, though! You know what they say about things that run in the family on the female side. Looks and temperament, my dear cousin. I pity you if you end up with a house full of daughters one day!"

"I never thought I would say this, but I wouldn't mind that in the slightest."

"Good to hear! Great-Uncle and I will expect a house full of nieces and nephews! Lord knows he won't get any children from me."

"You'll find the right person one day, Sal. I never thought meeting someone I was more than just physically attracted to would ever happen. It's hard to explain, but when it happens, you know it in an instant."

Sal glances down at his phone just as mine buzzes with an incoming message. I chuckle out loud and look up at my cousin, who's shaking his head. "Well, it seems at this very moment your sweet little girlfriend is still causing the entire security team more than a pile of grief."

I can't help but smile at the thought of their chastisement. "Nick and Cole deserve a bit of it, though, for taking her to the plane without talking to me first," I say, still pissed beyond words at the entire situation we find ourselves in.

"Jay's calling in. Can you deal with the home situation?" I ask Salvatore, who nods and gets on the phone to call Great-Uncle.

I hit Jay's contact number. "Jay here," he says.

"Any word on the Dominic situation?"

"Nothing yet, Giovanni. I know you're anxious to have him out of the picture, but I need to ask you a favor. I know you have connections that can reach into the prison where he's being held, but please don't do anything rash. We need to find out who else he has working for him and if someone else is pulling his strings. If we don't, they're going to keep coming."

I know what he's really saying. Keep the bastard alive. "I'll give the team some time, but not much. In one snap of my family's goddamn fingers, he will be dead. We've only held out this long to get some answers, but no more," I say, causing Salvatore's eyebrows to raise at my directness and change in temperament.

"I understand," Jay says. "The good news is that we've been able to tap into the feds' communication lines. They have their eyes and ears on Mancini too. They haven't been able to pinpoint who he has working for him either, though. We've also been running under the assumption that since he broke off with the Chicago family, and then got turned out by yours, he was calling the shots. What if he's on the receiving end of the orders, instead of giving them? Think about all the fire and manpower involved, the drones, and the tenacity. If we take Mancini out now, we'll never know who to watch out for until it's too late," Jay says.

"You don't need to convince me further." Everything is starting to come together. The cousins who turned against the family were already working for Mancini long before he got caught skimming money from the Chicago Mafia. It never made any sense to me that the cousins would jeopardize their position with the family for what seemed small potatoes, extorting money from low-income families. Seems that's just the tip of the iceberg, and if someone else is pulling the strings, and the cousins thought they would have their backing when it came time to put a stop to Uncle Carlos' vision for the expansion in Vegas, or even me moving into position as Don when Great-Uncle passes, it makes a hell of a lot more sense.

"As much as I want him dead, I completely agree with the strategy that you're using, and until now, if I'm being honest, I wasn't so sure. I'm still pissed as hell that Serena got caught in the middle of this war, but I know that you'll keep her safe and get to the bottom of it. Just do it soon, Jay. This is fucking killing me, capiche?"

"Roger that," he says, his answer for just about everything when he means okay.

"Does your intel have any update on the communication tap they were able to get in place on my cousin's line?" I ask Jay, because it's already been twelve hours since we found out Mancini was the traitor in the family, and my patience is growing thinner by the minute.

"We have a tap on everything going through that wire, but nothing yet, Gio. As much as I hate what we had to put you and your family through, we needed those damn numbers. Our intel group is working round the clock to monitor and decipher all the traffic. They're good at what they do, the best around the globe. We'll get to the bottom of it."

I nod, because while I may not like it, I do understand that these things can take time. "Just get it figured out quickly. In the meantime, tell me what's happening at home with Serena. I understand she's not taking the news about staying at the Larussio estate too kindly."

It's Jay's turn to laugh out loud. "That's a huge understatement. Let's just say the team is earning their money right now. Serena is pissed that we took her to your home on your say-so and didn't confer with her first. She's worried, probably rightfully so, that her nonna will hit the roof when she finds out that she's being placed in a home of the Larussios. They haven't had a chance to explain to her that you have separate guest villas set up for each of her brothers' families and that her nonna and her nurse will share a villa of their own. Oh, and she's also concerned your great-uncle and her nonna will go head to head."

I laugh at that. "Well, she's probably not too far off the mark there, but my great-uncle cares about Serena. There was a time he wouldn't have allowed any of her family on the estate. He's not only permitted it, but has actually arranged the accommodations himself.

It will all sort itself out. One thing, though, Jay. I don't think Great-Uncle's aware that her brothers have hidden their wives and children. Let's keep it that way. I don't want him to worry any more than he already is. Your security team hasn't been able to find them, so they've done a great job getting them off the grid. I just want to make sure that we find them before Mancini's crew does. We both know they have people scouring the countryside for anyone who means anything to a Larussio. Time is of the essence!"

"I'll double the efforts on that front and call her oldest brother myself to see if I can convince him that we're trying to keep them protected."

"Good. In the meantime, make sure Serena and her brothers are comfortable and that she is able to help console her nonna as she transitions to the estate. I'll deal with the rest when I land," I say, disconnecting and glancing up into the dark narrowed eyes of Salvatore, who has just stalked back into the cabin.

"We need to call the entire family, as well as the security team. One of the cousins just got wind that Serena's brothers have hidden their family with a small gang of rivals in the north. We know where they are. Unfortunately, so does Mancini's group. The security intel team just picked up the chatter over the wires. You good with having our men go in without going through protocol?"

"Hell yes. I told her we would safeguard her entire family. Damn it! Have them protected at all costs," I roar, because Serena will never forgive me or any of my family if something happens to her family. "And find out how they knew where they were!"

"The same way they knew everything else. Our fucking cousin. Intel got positive confirmation, and if he wasn't already dead, he would be now!" Salvatore growls, pounding a message onto the screen of his phone. "They're going into the safe house now and will bring them to our estate. I told them to do it as easy as they can since there are women and children involved."

I text Jay with an update and look at the message he returns.

> Got word about the same time as you. Agree
> with the plan. Stand by.

I nod, knowing that I'm going to need to bring Great-Uncle up to speed now. "No time like the present to share the good news with Great-Uncle," I say to Sal, who raises his eyebrows at me and slides his tall, muscular frame into the armchair across from me. I sigh as I connect and place my cell on speaker and put it on the table in front of us.

"What the hell is going on? I am still the Don of this goddamn family, Giovanni," my great-uncle roars.

Chapter 5

Serena

That man infuriates me like no one else on earth! How dare he not respond to my message after everything that has transpired? I've waited at least ten whole minutes, and that's ten minutes too long in my book! My fingers are just itching to hit the connect button so I can hear his voice and yell at him for having his security men take me to his home instead of where I planned to go with my family.

I am just about ready to type him a message, give him a sound piece of my mind, when my cell plays Giovanni's ring tone. I let it sound once, then twice. I contemplate giving him a taste of his own medicine and letting it go to voicemail, but I can't because I desperately need to hear his voice, even if I am pissed as hell at that man right now!

"Hello!"

"Tesoro, I thought you would know by now that I make the rules, I control your pleasure, and keep you safe. You do not leave, go off on your own, and put yourself in danger. You haven't had a punishment spanking yet, but you are certainly deserving of one," Giovanni says, and the sound of his voice and his threat makes my center pool with desire even though I am madder than hell at this man. Just thinking about his form of correction makes my thighs tighten with need, but this is about my family's safety, and I can't back down.

"You were right, Giovanni. You were always right. Every single one of my family is in peril because I love you. How could either of us live with ourselves if something happened to the people I love? Think about my brothers' families. My sister-in-laws, my nieces, and nephews, even my unborn nephew? They are innocent. They have done absolutely nothing, but your rivals will use my family to get to me, and ultimately to you. What if they had really taken my nonna? I would have given myself over to the enemy to ensure that she was not harmed, and then they would have gotten exactly what they wanted."

"Serena, they will not get to you or your family."

"If it were just me, I could do it, but it's not. Mancini's men could take any of my family knowing that I would do anything they demanded in order to keep them safe. The security men can't be everywhere all the time. Your enemies will always be looking for a chink in the armor. One day they will find it, Giovanni, and when they do, I will have to give myself up because I can't live with myself if they hurt my family. In the end they will end up torturing or killing me and hurting you. You warned me; I just didn't fully understand until I heard the conversation in the bathroom. I thought they had my nonna, Giovanni. You can't imagine the terror I felt."

"I know the fear you talk about. Every single time I imagine them getting their hands on you or anyone of your family, I feel that fear! I tried to walk away, to do the right thing, but it's far too late for that now, tesoro. They know you are protected by the Larussios, and they know you are mine. The family wouldn't be protecting you otherwise, and they know it. The only way they can fully protect you is to ensure you are surrounded by our intel and security teams and have you stay at our estate. It is virtually impenetrable."

"I know, Giovanni, it's just so much to take in, and they will all be furious with me."

"Great-Uncle has even personally been overseeing the guest house preparations to make sure everything on the property is ready for your family. Your nonna, brothers, and their families will have a safe place to live and will all be protected by the family until this is over. You will be safe, and your family will be safe, capiche?" Giovanni asks, and that husky voice of reason has a calming effect on the anxiety I feel.

Time and time again he comes to me and my family's rescue, and time and time again we reject him, but yet he continues to give so much. My sense of shame only deepens as I consider what he must have gone through when I left, but he must know by now that my family will never accept him. The family has always been the cause of my family's heartache, and that will never change.

"Tesoro, say something. I know you're upset, but everything has been arranged for their safety and comfort. Your nonna and each of your brothers will have a separate guest house. Great-Uncle has been giving staff instruction to get things prepared," Giovanni says.

I wipe the tear that silently falls. "Great-Uncle has been doing that?"

"Indeed, tesoro. You have become very special to many of the Larussios. Now, do as I ask. Make sure your nonna is comfortable and your brothers know you are not being held against your will. They are concerned about your well-being and that of their families. If it makes you feel any better, Jay's team is working around the clock to reunite them with their wives and children. It will not be long," Giovanni says.

The tears can no longer be contained. They spill from my eyes and over my cheeks. I swallow past the lump in my throat, taking a moment to compose myself enough to respond. "I love you so much, Giovanni. I don't know how I will ever thank you. The fact that all of your family is so supportive means the world to me."

Giovanni's great-uncle always seems so tough and staunch, but I've seen the softer side of him when he refers to his deceased wife or his son. They were both taken at an early age, leaving Giovanni as the oldest nephew in line as Don of Italy, and it's clear to see how much he loved them when he talks about them. Great-Uncle has shown that same caring side to me, and he has earned a special spot in my heart right along with his great-nephew.

"I have to take a call, tesoro, but I will be thinking of you until I see you again," Giovanni says before disconnecting.

The driver pauses briefly as the car reaches the intimidating entrance of the Larussio estate. The armed guards who protect the property must be expecting us, because the gates open, and they wave us through immediately. Nick and Cole are on their cells, doling out instructions as we drive along the winding road that eventually leads us to the main villa. The driver uses the semi-circle driveway and pulls up to the front door, where Great-Uncle is standing to greet us.

"Let me out," I say to Cole, who has the left side of the backseat blocked with his mammoth body. I know better than to get out of the left side of the car by myself. Always, always, the side that allows the car to block me from a distance.

Cole is busy texting and nodding to the person he's talking to, but he hasn't taken his eyes off me and holds up a finger, gesturing me to wait a second. After a few brief moments, he disconnects. "We're cleared; we can go now," Cole says, sliding his phone in his pocket as he opens the door and helps me get out of the backseat. I wonder in passing if perhaps he will tell Giovanni that I do pay attention to the rules, at least the ones that make sense.

"Thanks, Cole," I say, sliding out to greet Giovanni's intimidating great-uncle, who is watching me with those hooded dark eyes as I approach.

This man, the Don of Italy, a man I grew up fearing, has put aside his precious protocols for me and my family. He closes the distance between us in two steps, pulling me into his arms. "You scared the entire family half to death, Serena. You don't ever leave on your own without clearing it with the family. You do not go against protocol, young lady!" Great-Uncle says, kissing me on both cheeks before giving me another squeeze as he continues to chastise me for my behavior.

This man, the one who for years was the root of all my nonna's fears, and mine as a result, has come to mean something to me too. I hug him back, hiding my tears in his chest, but he lifts my face and wipes them with his thumb. "You, your nonna, and your brothers are safe. You are protected by the family. We are going for your brothers' families as we speak. Come, let's talk inside," Great-Uncle says, guiding me through the large entryway and into the great room. "Would you like a glass of wine while we wait for your nonna?"

I nod. It's early, but a glass of my favorite red sounds excellent. The attendant hovering nearby pours each of us a glass and brings them to us before leaving the room. I swirl my drink, needing the moment to inhale the complex bouquet before taking a small sip of the red made exclusively for the family from their own vineyards. "It's divine," I say to Great-Uncle, who nods his agreement and smiles broadly.

"Indeed. It was a new crop, and we're exceptionally pleased."

"I knew the family owned vineyards, but I guess I didn't realize your family was in the wine-making business until Giovanni mentioned it on our trip to the States. This is truly exquisite," I say, taking another small sip.

"The family has branched out in many ways over the years. Giovanni has a multitude of high-end hotels and resorts. Many of the cousins have different business ventures all over this country and America. Carlos will now have the most elite resort in America's adult playground, and I don't like to brag, but the Larussios' vineyards have become the leading supplier for many wineries across the globe. Of course, we keep the premium grape for our own label," Great-Uncle says, referencing the red wine we hold in our hands.

Great-Uncle glances down at his phone and grimaces. "Serena, the security team has just brought your nonna onto the property. I fear she will be upset without you to console her," he says.

"Please, don't take it personally, but she most definitely will be disgruntled. Is Gracie, her nurse, with her?" I ask.

"Her nurse?"

"Yes, Giovanni has been paying a private nurse to care for her, and Nonna's become quite attached to Gracie. She even reads to Nonna when I'm not around to do it myself," I say.

"She's here," he says, seemingly cautious. "I just didn't realize that she was your nonna's nurse. I was asked to give her clearance by Antonio."

I try to hide my smile, but nothing gets past this man, and he usually knows absolutely everything, a point of contention with both Giovanni and Salvatore. He grunts under his breath, but I see the slight curl of his lips even if he tries to disguise it from me, and now, I too am curious about whatever is happening between Gracie and Antonio.

Great-Uncle glances down at his phone. "Well that didn't take long. It would seem your nonna has arrived and is giving everyone a piece of her mind. Go and calm the woman. The security team is at a loss," Great-Uncle says, chuckling out loud while I place my almost untouched glass of wine on the table before heading to their rescue.

Chapter 6

Gio

Sal and I reach the estate, and we both try to conceal our amusement at the sight before us as we enter the great room. Serena should, by all accounts, be nervous around Great-Uncle after putting him in a position where he had to make a split decision to go against his protocols, but she's anything but. Instead, she sits sipping a glass of red with Great-Uncle as though nothing is amiss. I swallow past the lump in my throat and the fear I've felt since she left, relieved that she feels completely at ease in our home and with my family.

I walk toward her, and she stands, her hands twisting nervously in front of her. "I should apologize for all the grief that I gave you about bringing my family here. Nonna is fast asleep and safe," Serena says, looking up at me, clearly unsure of what reaction she will get.

"Come here, tesoro," I say, pulling her into my arms and hugging her tight. I'll deal with her disobedience and everything else later. She will learn to trust me and not take matters into her own hands, but right now I can't think about anything except crushing her in my strength and feeling her heartbeat against my chest.

Serena looks up at me with those doe-like deep brown eyes—the ones that held me captive from the start, the ones that are now filled with gold flecked emotion. "I'm sorry I ran instead of talking to you, Giovanni," she whispers so only I can hear.

I push her hair back to expose the sensitive creaminess of her neck. "You aren't to be punished yet, but you will be soon, tesoro," I whisper into the sensitive shell of her ear.

She turns her lust-filled eyes up at me. I stroke down the side of her neck, intending to calm the rapid pulse, but instead my touch accelerates it. My sweetheart is so responsive, her body wants mine even when her mind is telling her to run far, far away! If I were a better man, I'd have let her leave, allowed her to go to her brothers, and had my family protect her from afar. I briefly contemplate how I've handled this situation and realize that I may be more of a Larussio than I realized.

Great-Uncle clears his throat, and I realize that I've been holding Serena pressed tightly against me, just rocking her in my arms. "Giovanni, we need to talk about this situation, and it's best if Serena is not present."

I feel her body stiffen against me. While Serena may have become close to Great-Uncle in the weeks that she stayed with him and Salvatore, her entire adult life has been spent in fear of him, and her family's lives are at stake. She has a right to be apprehensive about a conversation that he wants to have without her present.

I shake my head. "I know it's against more protocol, but Serena has been through so much. She's just learning to trust us. Whatever we discuss, we do it with her present."

Salvatore's eyes are deep, dark, and hooded, giving nothing away. He and I are as close as brothers, and he has developed a respect and admiration for Serena. But women are not privy to heavy conversations; it is not only Great-Uncle's way, but the way of our world, the mafioso world. And Salvatore and I both know it.

Great-Uncle turns first to me, and then to Salvatore, just contemplating. Serena's body remains tense beside me. I draw her in, pulling her tight against me as reassurance. He does not miss a thing, and his eyes track the action. He registers Serena's discomfort, and after a long, uncomfortable silence, finally nods his assent. "She will stay, but only as far as we can assure her that she and her family will be safe. The details we will discuss alone, capiche?"

I nod, hoping to convey just what this gesture means to me. He returns the motion and then looks to Salvatore, who gives a curt nod of agreement.

"Very well," Great-Uncle says. "We have Serena's nonna in her cabin and Gracie, her nurse, has been brought in to care for her. All her medication, equipment, and a special bed have been placed in the cabin, just like the one that you had in the penthouse, Giovanni."

This man would normally be berating me about breaking protocol, not giving an inch, but instead has been on the phone to secure items for Serena's nonna, who has not been quiet about her abhorrence for me or my family. I glance to Salvatore. His lips have turned upward, but aside from that, he doesn't give any indication that Great-Uncle is saying anything out of the normal.

I turn to Great-Uncle, because the magnitude of his concession is not lost on me in the slightest. "I understand you were also personally dealing with all the cooking, cleaning, and housing arrangements before everyone arrived. I'm sorry everything landed in your hands to deal with."

"No apologies. We protect our family. Serena, though not officially, is family to us. We protect our own, and she knows this now if she didn't already," Great-Uncle says.

Serena leaves my arms and walks toward Great-Uncle. Sal and I watch with widened eyes as she reaches him and places her arms around his middle. "I am so sorry my family has brought so much trouble to your door, but I am so grateful for your family's protection. After what me and my nonna have been through, it means the world to me," Serena says, and we watch his arms fold around her and hug her tight.

Salvatore gives me an *I told you so* look. One that says, *if you ever plan on breaking up with this girl, you are going to have hell to pay.*

I smile widely, because after all the fear that Great-Uncle would never accept Serena or her family, this is the best gift in the world. When she is done hugging him, she pulls back and looks into his eyes. "The men are after me so that they can hurt Giovanni. I want every one of them dead. Will you help me?" Serena asks.

Sal's eyes widen, and I'm pretty sure they are a mirror image of my own. No one, not even our family, discusses so forthrightly plans such as this. She has just barely been cleared, and there is the very real possibility that Great-Uncle will now see her as a spy or a plant to get information that could bury the entire Larussio Family.

Great-Uncle eyes Serena for a moment and then quietly asks her to go and sit at the table while he has a word with his nephews. I watch the motion in her throat as she swallows, realizing that she has crossed a line, and then nods her agreement before taking a seat at the dining room table.

Great-Uncle gestures to the great room with his eyes, and Sal and I both follow him out of the room, and I close the door behind us. Nothing good will come of this, and the tightening in my chest is almost suffocating. No one outrightly asks the Don of Italy if he will help them kill people, unless they are undercover, because no one else would dare.

My jaw is locked tightly, because it is me, and no one else, who has brought this situation to the family. I don't know quite how this is going to shake out yet, but I won't have Serena or Salvatore accused of things that should fall squarely on my shoulders.

"The air is cool in here," Great-Uncle says, using code to ensure the room was swept for bugs as he points in a circle to the ceiling.

Salvatore nods. "It's clear, as always. I just got confirmation of a sweep about twenty minutes ago," he says.

"Very good. Giovanni, you must know how this looks. I have come to care for your girlfriend, admittedly, a great deal. She is genuine, she cares for you, and has even put herself through the ropes of self-defense with Salvatore and his goons, but let us not remember that her first loyalty is to her nonna, her brothers, and their families. That is why she ran, no?" Great-Uncle says, his dark eyes searching.

I can't argue and nod my agreement. "It is. She was running from me to ensure their safety. I was open with her about the fact that our enemies would come for her, torture her, in order to get to me. She didn't back down, but when Jay's team was working to flush Mancini's team out, they used shadow games and made Serena believe that her nonna was captive."

"They do not do this!" Great-Uncle roars. "We tell them what they can share with our women. We will not allow our women to be used as pawns. I will not have it!"

I would much rather not have Serena concerned with any of this, but Jay was right. It was necessary. Serena needs to be fully aware of what can transpire if she is to stay with me. It's that knowledge that kept her from running without alerting her security team. I take a deep breath inward, because convincing Great-Uncle of anything, much less something that goes against the most sacred of all of his protocols, the one that's been handed down from generation to generation, is daunting.

"I didn't approve of Jay's methods at first, but he did it for a reason. Apparently, Katarina gave the security team the slip when they were first getting to know her. She didn't fully understand their role or commitment to keeping her safe. She thought she would be better off without them and was almost killed as a result. Since then, they've been very conscious to ensure anyone they protect understands the risks."

"Need I remind you it did not work? Serena ran!" Great-Uncle roars.

"She ran because the loss of her nonna, or any of her family, is too much for her to even contemplate. It was just too much."

His eyes darken, and he starts to say something, but he has to hear me out. I raise my hand to ward off another onslaught of his wrath toward the security team. "I take solace in the fact that Jay and his team ensured that if she ever ran, she would do so with security. That's what's important here, her safety. She's not a plant, Great-Uncle. Her feelings are sincere, and I plan to marry her, with or without the family's blessing!"

He doesn't say a word for far too long. I inhale deeply, knowing this could go a multitude of ways. No one defies the Don of Italy, and certainly not in front of another family member.

"She means everything to me," I say to Great-Uncle.

He nods, taking it in and slowly contemplating. "She has given up her entire livelihood, gone against her family's wishes, denounced your wealth at every turn, and only left when she felt the need to protect her family. Her request of me only solidifies her commitment and dedication to her family and ours. In our hearts we know this, Giovanni, but you also know this is not enough. Protocol must prevail in this instant, capiche?"

Chapter 7

Serena

Giovanni's great-uncle seems to look right through me when I ask him for help. I know what needs to be done and that he and the family can help me, but his entire manner turns ice cold. Asking me to take a seat is just a polite way to let me know that I'm no longer privy to their conversation, and with that he turns abruptly, leaving me with only my thoughts and a bottle of red as Giovanni and Salvatore follow him out and close the door behind them.

I shouldn't have asked, I shouldn't have said a word, but I won't take it back! These people have already taken Nonna's home, her most prized possession. The tactic they are using now—trying to kill me or, worse, my family—to get to Giovanni leaves me absolutely no ability to stop them without the family's intervention. When I asked him outright, I clearly crossed a line—the invisible stripe that sent the men into a hushed meeting, presumably to talk about me and my family and what a burden we are to them.

I've managed to down two very generous glasses of wine before Giovanni walks into the room. The grim look on his face is something I haven't seen before and causes a shiver to run down my spine and goosebumps to raise on the back of my arms.

He looks at the almost empty bottle on the cabernet, and takes the half-empty glass in my hand from me, leaning past me to place it on the sideboard. "Tell my family what they want to hear," Giovanni whispers, so low that I can barely make it out before his great-uncle and Salvatore walk into the room.

I have learned not to fear the family over the last couple months, but they are solemn and scary as they gaze at me tonight. Salvatore stalks toward me—glancing at Giovanni, who nods his assent—before taking my hand. "You know we have become fond of you, but be that as it is, protocol demands that we ensure you aren't wired, Serena."

"I would never allow that," I say in protest.

Salvatore puts his finger to my lips. "Shh… I don't think any of the family believe that you would knowingly be tapped, but there are always ways to worm into our loved ones lives and set bugs in place. We have to be sure you weren't wired. It is protocol, relatively painless, embarrassing perhaps, but you must endure it."

I glance from him to Giovanni and then to his great-uncle, and both look solemn and remain silent.

"What do you plan to do?" I ask and not one of them looks me in the eye. They glance at the door as it opens, and a very tall, serious-looking blonde woman dressed in a red sweater, black skintight pants, and flat-heeled boots walks into the room.

She assesses me from a distance, her eyes cold and aloof. "Giovanni?"

He shakes his head at me and gives her a nod.

She walks toward me, and she and Sal both grasp my arms and lead me out of the great room, and I do nothing to stop it, although my heart is racing. Giovanni and his family are handing me over to this gangster woman. The fact that Giovanni let her take me without a word hurts deeply, but I don't have long to dwell on this as Sal opens a door off the kitchen that leads downstairs.

As soon as the door closes behind me, my blood turns cold. The lower level is where the Mafia always take their victims to be tortured, and every movie I've seen with those gruesome scenarios flash through my mind, and suddenly my feet stop moving. "Giovanni!" I scream.

Sal grasps me by the arms, turning me to him. "Serena, he can't hear you through the soundproofing, and he can't be with you right now. We need to check you for wires. Gretta will need to search you head to toe, and it will be embarrassing, but you have nothing to fear unless you're wired," Sal says, turning to leave me with the blonde Amazon.

I watch him make his way upstairs, and she turns to me. "We do this the easy way, okay? I give you instruction, and you do what I ask, and there's no harm."

I haven't been given much of a choice. I nod, trying to calm my fear, but my body is in fight or flight, and it's all that I can do to keep my teeth from chattering with fear.

"Strip, I will search you."

"I'm not undressing for you!"

"You will. We do it the easy or the hard way. Your choice, really," Gretta says, looking at me as though she has all the time in the world.

"I am not taking my clothes off for you! If Giovanni wants to see me completely humiliated, then you tell him to come down and do it his damn self! Now! Do it now!" I yell.

Amazon girl takes out her phone and sends a message. In a manner of moments, the door opens, and I watch as Giovanni's shoes become visible, and he makes his way down the stairs. "The search must be done, Serena. Would you prefer me to undress you or to give you instruction?"

I look from him to the blonde Amazon girl. "Make her leave, and I will do what you wish."

"Serena, if I tell her to leave, we need to turn the cameras on. Having a female do this is a luxury extended to you because we care about you. No cameras, but someone the family trusts."

"Are you serious; these are the rules?"

He gives me one curt nod, his eyes intense and solemn. "You will do as we ask. It will be quick and painless, but as Salvatore mentioned, it is embarrassing. Perhaps we can make it a bit more fun if I give the instruction," Giovanni says, winking at me and glancing up at the roof.

Then I see the cameras. They are strategically placed in every corner of the room. I'm contemplating whether they have audible capability when Giovanni answers my unspoken question by glancing at them again and then back to me. "Serena, do it now."

"You want me to strip with her in the room?" I ask, looking at the long, golden haired Amazon who's standing by the doorway and patiently waiting.

"Strip, Serena, everything."

I look to him, and then to her, and he gives me a nod, gesturing me to do as he's instructed. I tentatively begin unbuttoning my blouse, but he is impatient. "We do not have all night, Serena. Shed your clothing and show me you're not wired," Giovanni says, and again he glances upward.

He's giving me all the clues. He is impatient to have this over and worried about the cameras being turned on if I do not comply. I nod, letting him know without words that I know exactly what he needs me to do. I may appreciate the fact that he's trying to keep me protected from the cameras, but I don't have to be one damn bit happy about the mortification of stripping in front of this gangster woman. "You want to humiliate me, make me strip for you?" I ask, unbuttoning the next button.

His deep brooding eyes track my every single movement, but he still doesn't say a word, which pisses me off to no end!

"You want everyone in this house to see what used to be yours, Giovanni, so be it," I say, divesting myself of my blouse one pearl button at a time. I toss the material to the floor leaving me in my sheer pink bra.

His eyes darken, and his jaw tightens as he watches me. "All your clothes, Serena."

"It's not enough to see that I don't have wires strapped to my chest. You need to see underneath my bra too?" I say, rubbing my hands over my chest and across my abdomen, because now the alcohol has fueled my anger. "Or perhaps you want to see something else; maybe you want to look at my pussy," I say, shimmying out of my pants, panties and all. "Maybe I have a wire inside; is that what you want your girly to check? Oh, wait, maybe we should have her check my ass too. Stick her fingers inside of what you say is only yours, see if I'm hiding a wire that you already know I'm not! This is your plan, Giovanni Larussio?"

He starts to say something, but I interrupt him. "Come here, girly," I say to the blonde as I walk toward her and the bench beside her. "I know what you want me to do," I say, bending over so that my naked ass is exposed to Giovanni's gaze. "You do exactly what you need to ensure that the family knows I'm not wired, and when you're through, I'm walking right out that fucking door!"

Chapter 8

Gio

I watch my dark-haired beauty presented stoically before me and the intimidating blonde, who has her orders and nothing more. Serena's hair is draped over her shoulder, and I can see her rapid breathing even from here. She will go through with this, she will follow their fucking protocols, because that is what she believes she has to do, and until just this very moment, so did I. The other option is to disregard the protocols and walk away, walk away from this life that continues to put Serena in danger and now subjects her to this. She does not deserve to be treated this way, and the anger I've tried to keep bottled up for years will no longer be contained.

I am just about to intervene and stop this entire thing when my great-uncle's voice bellows through the intercom system with one word: "Enough."

Serena has more than passed the test.

"Leave us!" I say, dismissing Gretta with a nod and waiting until she's upstairs and has closed the door behind her. I walk toward Serena's hunched frame still bent over the bench, pressing the button on the wall that will turn off the audio wired into the room. I run my hand down the smoothness of her back, massaging the tight and rigid muscles in an attempt to coax her upward. "Serena, it's over. You've more than passed the test, tesoro."

She doesn't raise up, though, and instead becomes very still. "Is she gone?"

"The audio is off, and she's gone, Serena. I'm so very sorry, tesoro. I didn't intend to let you go through with the search; he just stopped it sooner than I did. He's grown very fond of you. He didn't even want to subject you to the normal approach," I say, caressing her back.

She lets me stroke her for a moment, but then stands to face me, covering her breasts with her arms.

"This is what you and the family do to innocent people? I don't even want to know what the normal approach is, Giovanni!"

She has suffered so much at the hands of the family, and now this. "I wouldn't have let it gone much farther before calling it off," I say, purposely avoiding her question about the normal protocol. "You weren't ever on camera, only audio, tesoro. You have come to mean a great deal to Great-Uncle, but he had to be certain," I tell her, not quite sure who I am trying to convince of this more.

The look she gives me is withering. "That Amazon woman, she really would have searched someone else? I was joking, a sick as hell joke, but you are serious!"

My jaw tightens. "You want me to lie to you or tell you the truth?"

"Tell me the truth, Giovanni. God! This family has always messed with my head! You know that, yet I am subjected to this while you do nothing to stop it! That's bad enough, but what are the others subjected to? Tell me!"

I can't tell her everything and run my hand through my hair in frustration. "The family knows that you are mine, and as such, you were provided certain protections, and that's why we had a female in the room for you."

Serena's eyes darken, and she slaps me square across the face. "You and your family! Disgusting!" she says, turning from me to walk toward her clothes that were left in a heap on the floor.

I rub my cheek where the fresh imprint of her hand is still

heated and fresh and watch her bend down and slip into her panties, and my cock hardens. She may be mad as hell at me, but he doesn't care. He wants her anyway. "Serena."

She ignores me, and I allow it, watching her in that position, letting her gather her blouse from the ground while my cock throbs in my pants. When she stands, she doesn't turn to me until she's fully covered herself. While my cock may have been tracking her body, my mind has been contemplating the very real possibility that this was simply too much for her.

She has done what it takes to be part of the family, but there are some things that she doesn't understand. I never should have told her that she got off lightly. Damn, she is pissed, and she doesn't even know the half of it! If this had been anyone but Serena, they certainly wouldn't have been afforded a woman. I am not the one in charge. This is how things have been handled for years, and maybe one day in the future it will change, but that day is not today.

Serena looks at me with those deep brown eyes that are usually either innocent and doe-like or filled with worry for her nonna and family, but this is neither; this is different. I've never seen the emotion that has settled into her eyes—pure anger, fury, and I try to gauge what else, perhaps outright revulsion?

"You asked the Don of Italy if he would kill someone for you. Tesoro, I know that you were only baring your heart and wishes because of your fondness for my family, but there are many others that would love to bring the family to their knees. The wires we were checking for are put in place every single day to try to do just that. The only way the family can mitigate the risk is to ensure strict protocols are in place when something like that transpires. You know in your heart that Great-Uncle didn't want to go through with it. So we found a different way to make sure any of the family questioning would know that you were not an agent or trying to get a drop on the family. That is all."

She looks at me with those deep brown eyes, but there's no light in them at all. I know what she's going to say before she even parts her lovely lips to speak, and my chest tightens as I swallow past the growing lump in my throat.

"We are too different, Giovanni. I thought I could fit into your life, but you will always have to follow the family's direction. It could not have been more clear tonight," Serena says, turning.

"Serena, if you are going to walk away, you at least need to hear me out."

"What, Giovanni? What can you possibly have to say that would help me forget this night and what the family was going to ask me to do?"

"We didn't ask you to do it. That's what you are forgetting, Serena. I gave you the clues, to let you know it was a farce. I watched as you realized exactly that it was for show. How could you think for one minute I would allow anyone, the family or not, to subject you to that? My family cares about you. They found a way to ensure that any other family member who would question would know that we had done our due diligence to protect the family, without actually going through with it."

She nods, and I think I might be getting through to her. "It was humiliating, but you're right; I did know it was a farce. I understood the clues this time, Giovanni. I know that you love me and knew that you weren't going to let it go too far. That much I understand, but what you don't understand is that it doesn't matter. The fact that if it had been anyone but me, they would have put some other poor woman through the humiliation of having a man actually search their most private parts to ensure they weren't traitors is appalling to me. I can't wrap my brain around it, Giovanni. You just accept it as routine and the family protocol."

How the hell do I explain this to her when it's been just one of the things that I haven't been able to reconcile myself for years. The ways of the family are part of the reason I ventured out on my own, built a legitimate empire. "Serena, you have to believe me when I tell you that I don't condone this treatment, of you or anyone else."

"Then why did you let it go on at all?" she cries, turning and poking me in the chest.

I capture her hand, the one that's intending to poke me again, before bringing it to my lips. "Serena, you know better. You weren't compromised. You had the power. You knew far before you opened your blouse that how you went about ensuring the family knew you weren't a threat was up to you. Tell me you didn't know that," I demand.

She looks down, and then after a few long moments, which I give her, she nods. "You are right. I did know because you gave me the clues. You're right, I did have a choice, and I could have handled it in a multitude of ways, but that doesn't excuse you or the family! They have no right to demand anything of anyone, and yet they do! Do you see how sick this is? Do you understand the reason that I can't be with you, Giovanni?"

Chapter 9

Gio

As she walks up the stairs and out of my life, it takes everything that I have not to bring her kicking and screaming back to my arms. I will myself to remain calm and give her this space after all that she has been through.

I send Sal a text to ensure Serena is taken to her family when they are shown to the property, and almost immediately my phone lights up with his incoming call.

"Nate just took Serena to her cabin, and her family is just starting to arrive. She asked Nate to drive her back to the airport in the morning. She made a call on the ride over and lined up a job with the air service she works for. I looked into her a little bit when you first became involved, and as you can imagine, she's the first choice for a service attendant on anyone's flight. No drama, classy, and always exceptional service is what I see on the reviews, over and over."

"I don't doubt that for a minute," I say.

"Giovanni, you need to do something, or she will be gone tomorrow. She needs a driver at 4 a.m. to get her to the private airstrip. She is adamant about leaving and going back to work. We need a game plan," Salvatore says.

I shake my head as though he can see me through the phone, because the words just don't come quite yet. After all that I have put her through, and all that she has shared with me, there is no possibility that I can hold her back. If she wants to leave, if she feels so strongly about needing to leave, then far be it from me or anyone in the family to hold her against her will. "Let her go, Sal. Make sure that Jay and his team are safeguarding her, but the family, we do nothing."

"You can't be serious. Giovanni, have you lost your fucking mind? She doesn't know what's best for her—you do!" Salvatore explodes.

"I thought I did, Sal, but instead I ended up finishing us. She doesn't want anything to do with me or the family. She can't get past the fact that we put her to a test. She knows that if we didn't care about her it would have been way worse. It's my fault. She told me she wanted to know everything, all eyes in, and I promised her nothing
less."

"So, she saw the truth, and it's too much," Salvatore says. "Great-Uncle's looking for an update. He's been pacing the floors since the ears went silent after you turned off the intercom."

"Well, how about we tell him the truth? She saw the monsters we are and left. Plain and simple," I say.

"You really believe that nonsense you're spewing? Our family protects all the people in our country from a multitude of issues. Deaths from horrible drugs infiltrating the country, all the trafficking; you name it, and we're fighting against it."

"Yeah, except when our family was extracting money from the most vulnerable in our country. How do you explain that, Sal?"

"That is a grave and horrendous tragedy, one which will take a great deal of time to make right, but we will do it, Giovanni. Even as we speak, our people are working to find each and every family that was blackmailed under our name, and we will make it right, no?"

"Sal, I know you're working diligently on this, and I should care more, but I just don't. Right now, I just need eyes on Serena. I know the security team have her under surveillance, but I need to make sure that someone in the family is watching out for her too."

"I'll do whatever you need, Gio, but at some point, we're going to sit down and talk about the family, the good we do in this country and its future," Salvatore says.

"We will, but right now I just need a little time," I say, disconnecting and heading to my room. The very place I should be sharing with Serena. How, in less than an hour, things can go from great to absolute shit, I will never know. That's not really true, because I do know. It's this family; it's the shadow of the Larussios, never far and always lurking.

I strip out of my suit and throw on my running gear before heading downstairs to pound out my frustration on the treadmill. I never should have told her that other women would have been subjected to far more humiliation during a search. Hell, I didn't even have a chance to tell her that those women were undercover, trying to get a drop on the family by cozying up to one of the men in the family, not that it would have made any difference.

In the end, what I told her was honest. She deserves that if she's going to be part of this family, and now she knows the truth. Well, not entirely the whole truth. I didn't tell her that those women probably didn't make it out alive. I'm usually spared even base knowledge about these things, but I do know that if this family thinks you are a traitor or are trying to get any information that could be used to bring harm or prison to the family, you will not live.

My phone buzzes with an incoming call from my great-uncle. Damn it all to hell! An hour on this fucking machine, and I'm still wound as tight as a drum and in no mood to discuss Serena with him right now. I send the call to voicemail and slow the machine before heading to the weights. I'm resting in between sets when I look up into the mirror on the wall and see my great-uncle standing in the door frame of the gym behind me. "We need to talk, Giovanni."

I sit up on the weight bench and turn to face him. "What do we need to discuss? She's made her decision. She's gone."

"I forbid it, Giovanni!"

"No disrespect intended, but you can't just fix this by forbidding it. I never should have allowed the test. Never! But I did, and that's on me. I'll have to live with that decision for the rest of my life. Every goddamn time I think about Serena, I will have to wonder what the hell ever possessed me to agree to your fucking protocols!"

His dark eyes narrow at me. "Come, Giovanni, was it the test? Because I think Serena knew exactly what she was doing, knew that she was being tested. No?"

He sees too goddamn much for his own good and for mine, or Sal's been flapping his fucking lips to the old man. "I told her she got off light, and she wanted to know the truth about what really happens to others in the same situation."

He looks incredulously at me. "Giovanni, what did you tell Serena?"

"The truth, I told her the fucking truth! That if she weren't protected by us, she would have been subjected to far worse humiliation, and it wouldn't have been at the hands of a woman by any fucking means of the imagination. Just that alone had her running out of here, scared out of her mind. What do you think would have happened if I had told her everything? Should I have told her that if anyone else had asked you to kill for them they would've been lucky to make it out alive? Maybe she would have felt better about that? No?"

"Enough, Giovanni!"

"No, she asked me for the truth. She needs to know the truth, and I need to give her time to process. Would you prefer she find out how our family operates after we've been married, and everyone has gotten far closer to her? Perhaps when children are involved?"

Great-Uncle starts to say something, but I'm just not in the mood and interrupt him before he can get a word out. "If she's unable to accept the realities of this family, then she can walk away. I will allow it, and she will remain under the protection of the family," I say.

"You seem to have forgotten that you are not yet the Don, Giovanni, and those decisions are not yours to make."

"This is my call to make. She has done nothing but love this family, but it is just too much for her. She has plans to leave the estate tomorrow, and our family will allow it because she needs time, and we will protect her! We will call the family and security together later in the day and put a plan in place to keep her safe from the time she leaves the estate."

Great-Uncle's eyes gleam with moisture, and he shakes his head. "If you would just stop talking and talking and just listen. It is too late. She has taken matters into her own hands. She is already gone, Giovanni, Serena is already gone."

Chapter 10

Serena

Nate is a good man, one of the many security agents who protect the family and those they care about. Salvatore has arranged for him to give me a ride to the cabin my family, and I are supposed to stay in, which is located somewhere on this vast property. I also know that he is loyal, and not to me, but that little piece of knowledge will work in my favor. I purposely call my employer while he's focused on driving but within earshot, and accept a new assignment to provide service for a flight to Paris the next day, and then I ask him to drive me to the airstrip the following morning at 4 a.m.

I know exactly when Nate has divulged this information to his employers, because Sal's ringtone immediately lights up my phone. Salvatore Larussio may be feared and revered by all of those who don't know him personally, but he has become as close as a brother to me. It makes me sad to ignore his call, but he is part of this family who does these despicable things. There is no way to reconcile the way the Larussios treat people, after what I learned. I was fortunate. I knew Giovanni would only allow it to go so far, even before Great-Uncle intervened, but what about the other women? What about their humiliation when these men make them strip and then search them in places that only lovers should see? They aren't even given the decency of having a woman do it. Horrible, unforgivable!

Nate walks with me from the car to the cabin, where I am greeted by my brothers, who have a multitude of questions about why they've been brought back to the Larussio estate. They should be happy that they are being protected, but sadly that is not the case, and they continue to fire question after question at me. They will never truly be friends of the Larussios. I try to answer all of them, but I am simply too exhausted and beg a brief time out in order to freshen up and make a few calls.

When I return, Sal has arrived and is talking with Nate. He looks like he's about to say something to me too, but he glances around at my brothers and decides it's probably not a very good idea. I have no doubt they have been bombarding him with questions in my absence. It's not long before he leaves, presumably to flap his loose lips to that no-good Giovanni. Well, he can flap all he wants, because little does he know that he will be doing exactly as I wish.

I let my brothers and Nate know I'm going for a walk and make my way into the fresh air. The estate is like a fortress, so the security team can let their guard down while we are within these walls, but still I make sure no one is watching before heading toward the car that brought my brothers and is still parked in the driveway. The driver is down the lane having a quick smoke break. With one more glance around to make sure I'm not seen, I quietly open the back door of the sedan. I shrug out of my light jacket and lay uncomfortably across the bottom of the backseat floor, pulling the jacket over the top of me. If someone passes by and looks down into the window, all they will see is a crumpled old jacket lying in the backseat of the car.

I hear voices talking, and they are getting closer. I hold my breath, waiting to see if I'll be found, fearful that one of the security team might have seen me, but the voices pass right by the car. Sal and Giovanni probably have them all so busy looking for the people who are after us that they didn't even see me slip out. They are trying to do everything in their power to protect me, and here I am running away. I am positive they will catch hell from Giovanni for this, but I have to leave. I have to get some distance, some perspective in my life, and I simply cannot stay!

The driver's door opens. I feel the seat move with the man's weight as he settles into the car. The door slams closed, the engine starts, and the vehicle begins moving, and I slowly let out the breath I have been holding.

It is about an hour later when the car slows and veers to the right. It then makes another turn, and I hear the crunch of gravel under the vehicle's wheels. Wherever we are going, it's off the beaten path. I wait as we come to a complete stop, and the driver gets out. I remain a while longer, just waiting to make sure the coast will be clear, before sitting up to reach for the car door handle.

I push it open as gently as I can and put one foot out, and then another, still somewhat squatting behind the door. I peek through the window to see if anyone is around. I survey my surroundings. We're in the middle of absolute nowhere, and it appears the driver has gone into the cabin that stands in front of us.

What the hell am I supposed to do now? Clearly this was not well thought out at all. I'm not even sure how many miles we are from the highway. It seemed to take forever since we slowed and veered off the main highway, and even the gravel road took some time. I hate to think how long it would take to get back to the main highway by foot. I'm still looking around when a silver gleam coming right from the ignition catches my eyes.

I glance closer and close the back passenger door quietly and walk duck-like around the back of the car until I reach the front driver's side door and open it. He's either not worried about the theft of this car, or he's just made a quick stop and will be back out to the car any minute. In which case I need to move my ass.

I slide into the driver's seat and close the door quietly before turning the ignition. I hit the gas just as the driver runs out of the cabin, screaming for me to stop.

I wave my hand in the air, and he's still chasing, but by now, he's becoming a small dot in the rearview mirror.

Now I have to think. I just need space, away from the Larussios and away from anyone who takes orders from the Larussios. I can't go back to my job tomorrow. That was just to throw Sal off my trail because I'm pretty sure they have my phone tapped. Well, I'm not going to use it, so they won't get any information that way, and I have plenty of cash in my purse to last me for a little bit.

I drive for a little while, and once I get on the highway, I push a button on the navigation screen to find hotels in the area. I'm definitely out in the middle of nowhere. I know a little bed and breakfast that usually has room and whose owner won't ask any questions, and that's the location I key into the GPS and where I head.

It's a long drive, and I turn the radio on to distract myself as I make my way up the coast. The coastal area is alive and vibrant with colorful houses built into the lush green hilltops looking down over the blue-green sea. The sun is warm, and I roll down the window a bit to let the warmth envelop my skin as I inhale the fresh air.

When I arrive in town, it's bustling as usual. I make my way to the local shopping area, and in less than an hour I have enough clothes and essentials to make it through a few days.

I drive to the bed and breakfast and pull into the driveway. When the owner sees the car, she comes out. Mrs. Caruso is a rotund lady with long, dark hair, which she usually keeps wrapped in a bun that sits high on her head.

"Serena, I didn't recognize you in that car," she says, taking in the expensive black sedan.

"It's not mine; it's on loan," I say, which is not really a lie. I am just borrowing it. It's just that they don't know it yet, but I do plan to return it, so not a lie, really. "Would you happen to have a spare room for a couple of days?" I ask.

"We do; in fact, we have three open right now. Pull the car into the back of the property, and then come in through the rear porch. I'll meet you there," Mrs. Caruso says, heading back into the house.

Perfect. This car stands out like a sore thumb, and the Larussios have men all over this country. I pull into one of the back stalls and throw the keys into my purse, grab my purchases, and head into the house. The kitchen is lively, with a few guests sitting around a large table, just finishing a meal. Everyone is friendly, and Mrs. Caruso asks if I'd like a glass of fresh lemonade or a glass of wine. Everyone knows that her lemonade is to die for. "Lemonade, please."

"If you want to put your things up, your room is at the top of the stairs, last one on the right. You have a beautiful balcony area and view of the coast from there."

"That sounds wonderful. I'll just go drop my packages off and be back down for a drink then." When I get to my room, it is every bit as nice as everything in and around the home is. Absolutely serene and just what I need to quiet the voices that won't shut down in my mind. I freshen up a little bit and then head downstairs, taking the offered glass of lemonade. I visit with the folks around the table for a short bit, but I am anxious to get back upstairs and do the inevitable. While I need time to myself, I do not want Giovanni and his family or the security team to worry about me.

Mrs. Caruso refills my glass, and I take it with me upstairs and out to the balcony, sliding out of my shoes so that I can feel the warmth on my toes. I pull out my cell and turn it on. Beep after beep with messages come through. Giovanni, Salvatore, my brothers, Jay, and Nate. I skim through Giovanni's, the first ten or so telling me to call him right away, at least to let them know that I am okay, until I get to the very last one, and tears fill my eyes as I read it.

> Let us know that you are safe. I will not
> come for you. You have my word.

I stare at his message for a long time and then type out a reply.

I am safe. I need time and space. Please let everyone know I am fine.

Absolutely no reply.

I don't know what I thought would happen, but this wasn't it. I thought he would come after me, at least send someone for me. I should be happy; this is what I wanted, after all. I need time to process, to get away from him and his family so that I can see things clearly. Nonna was right; the things the Larussios do are bad. They humiliate, hurt, and kill people. How much blood does Giovanni have on his hands? I know for certain he gave the order to have his two cousins murdered. How many more? I don't know what they did with Sammy, the other cousin who was in charge. Who knows what they did with him after they got this confession.

Giovanni did that, I know that he did, and why didn't it bother me? Because he was defending me? Because it was righting a wrong? What makes it okay to take another life, play God like that? And how am I any different? I asked Great-Uncle to kill for me—exactly what started this. What would Nonna think of her precious granddaughter now, if she only knew? If only I had kept my thoughts to myself, none of this would have happened, but I didn't.

I take a sip of my lemonade and continue to gaze out at the sea for a very long time, allowing the tears to fall. Giovanni, why do I love you so much?

Chapter 11

Gio

The fear that seizes my heart when Great-Uncle tells me Serena is gone is like nothing I have ever felt. "What do you mean?" I ask, standing from the weight bench.

"She's gone; she left the estate. That's all I know; that's what I've been trying to tell you. You wouldn't answer your phone. I'm so sorry; this is all my fault. My goddamn protocols!"

"Goddamn it!" I yell. "When? How long? Where the fuck is our security team?" I say, glancing down at my phone, the one I had turned off and now is blowing up with beep after beep of a multitude of messages. I scan them all quickly and then inhale deeply.

"This woman is going to be the living death of me!" Great-Uncle says.

"Security has her!" I say, and I immediately see Great-Uncle's shoulders visibly relax. Who knew she would come to mean so much to my entire family in such a short time?

"We should head straight to the great room. Jay and his team were heading to the house when he sent this message. They are probably already upstairs with Sal," I say.

I go to walk past him, but his hand on my shoulder stops me.

"I'm sorry, Giovanni. It was my order, and it drove her away. I'm sorry."

I nod, taking a moment to form my words. "This is not on you. She is mine, Great-Uncle. This is on me. I know it's the family way, but going forward, where Serena is concerned, no one but me gives an order that affects her. Ever. I simply won't allow it in the future." I walk past him to open the door that will lead us upstairs.

The heavy living room drapes are open, and the sun is spilling in through the floor-to-ceiling windows. Sal, the security men, and all of Serena's brothers and a couple of our cousins are gathered and talking animatedly. Amelia, one of the kitchen servers, is doing her best to keep everyone hydrated with freshly squeezed lemonade and water.

Jay looks up from his phone, sees us walk in, and heads straight toward us. "She's fine, Gio. One of our best drivers is in the car with her. They were about half an hour out before he realized someone was in the back seat of his car. We let him know to go to one of your cabins tucked away in the countryside. They're about an hour from the cabin. We have teams in place following them, and they aren't too far behind them, and another crew is getting into place to surround the cabin just in case Mancini's men come out of the woodwork. The driver could have been anyone, could be taking her anywhere, for all she knows. I don't know what the hell she was thinking."

She wasn't. She was in shock and angry and upset. She needs time to process things I've told her. "Thank you for keeping her safe."

Jay nods. "We need a plan for when she arrives. We don't hold people against their will, but obviously we need to keep her safe."

"We do nothing. She left; she needs time. We give her that."

"No disrespect, but, Gio, she's going to be out in the middle of nowhere. We can't keep her in the cabin against her will, and if we just let her go, it's miles to the highway, and unless she plans to jumpstart the car somehow, she's not going to get very far."

"Tell the driver not to let on that he knows she's in the car. Have him leave the keys in the ignition. Then make sure your men keep her surrounded as tightly as a bubble, but no one goes near her. If you need triple the teams, pull them in. Spare no expense, but you keep that woman safe!"

"Gio," both Great-Uncle and Salvatore say at the same time.

I look from one to the other and shake my head because the words just don't come. All I can do is shake my head and turn, heading up to my room before anyone sees the emotion in my eyes. No, we don't go after her. The shit I said to her scared her so bad that she would rather be in the middle of nowhere without security, away from her family, than to be anywhere near me or my family right now, and she has earned that right.

It is over an hour later when Jay sends me a text letting me know that Serena is safe. She has taken the car and appears to be heading toward Naples, and they have eyes on her from all angles. She's heading toward the area she grew up, where things are familiar to her.

I've showered, shaved, and dressed, but my mood has not improved by the time I go downstairs. Her brothers are talking animatedly with Salvatore and my cousins about their families. Security seems tense and on the ready, like any minute all hell is going to break loose, and they may not be wrong.

All of their wives and children have been moved to the estate, and I knew we were going to have to provide them with answers at some point. I've seen these men when the women they love are in danger and so have my men. They drove a vehicle right through one of my goddamn cabins to get to their sister. It didn't make one bit of difference to them that we were the fucking Mafia and could have taken them out with one spoken order. Might as well get this shitstorm over with now!

I clear my throat as I walk into the room, and Sal looks as though he's about to throttle someone. I nod to her three brothers, Anzio, Aramis, and Corino. "Gentlemen, let's talk, have a drink, and I'll fill you in on what I know, and then we'll take it from there, no?" I say, gesturing to Amelia to bring wine. A little bit of red always seems to help with difficult conversations.

They continue to glare at me and Salvatore, but take seats

around the table and accept glasses of wine as it is served. "Men, I know it came as a shock to you to find out the Larussios went into the area that you had your family safeguarded in, but you have to know it was for their protection."

Anzio starts to say something, but Salvatore stops him. "Enough, at least hear what he has to say. Then you will have plenty of time to disagree," he says, and I can tell he's had about enough for one day, and I see my cousins nodding at Sal's reprimand.

"Fine, tell us how you found our families, and why you made war with the people who are trying to safeguard them for us? How do you expect us to explain what happened to them?"

I wait until he's finished, and Sal rolls his eyes skyward like he's been dealing with this shit for hours. "I understand, Anzio. Let me tell you what is happening, at least, as much as I can," I say.

He is sullen and angry but nods his agreement and takes a drink of his wine. This is not going to be an easy conversation, but they need to hear it straight if they're going to be any help at all to us.

"We learned that Dominic Mancini, who used to be Bernatelli's right-hand man, has given his crew orders to take Serena alive."

"The fucking Chicago boss that was behind embezzling money from Serena and Nonna, right?" Aramis says.

"Exactly. Bernatelli found out that Mancini was skimming money from the top and not giving him all of what was collected."

"And how does that have anything to do with us, with our families, with our children?" Corino asks, pushing his untouched wine glass in front of him away.

"Give me time, I'm getting there. I know this has not been easy for you and your families. If it's to make sense, you need to know the background. My family has been at odds with the Chicago Mafia for years. They are enemies of my Uncle Carlos in New York City, and as such, enemies of ours. Mancini caught wind that Bernatelli was onto the fact that he was skimming money and sought refuge with our family. We allowed him into one of our safe houses, at least until we learned he was trafficking. We then kicked him out, and because he didn't have protection, he got picked up shortly thereafter. We learned later the men who were working for him were the very same people extorting money from your sister and nonna, along with several members of our family."

I am prepared for the outburst, and it certainly doesn't take long. "All along it was the Larussios! How many years did my sister work herself into the ground to give your family money that wasn't owed!" Aramis yells.

I deserve that, and he's earned the right to get it off his chest, even though my cousins and Salvatore don't look like they agree. "It was the Larussio Family; that I cannot deny. We are still not sure how it happened, but we will learn. We do not condone trafficking in our country, and I was the one who outed him for that reason. He wants me to pay for his stint in prison," I say, hoping I don't have to go into the details, but that hope gets blown out of the water with Aramis' outburst.

"Nonna was right! It's always you Larussios! Every single time something tragic happens to our family, you are at the helm of it!" Aramis shouts, getting up from his seat. Nate is standing behind him and puts a hand on his shoulder, not saying a word, just letting him know with the gesture that he and my entire security team are standing right behind him.

He sits back down, empties his wine glass, and places it on the table with a thud. Amelia, ever the observant attendant, moves to his side of the room and replenishes his glass. "Tell me how your story ends with Serena leaving and your family starting a war with the people who were protecting my family and moving them here! Tell me what you want with them," Aramis says.

I let his comment sink in. Now, just now, do I realize what he and his brothers are thinking. They believe that I had their families snatched because Serena left. Now I understand the hostility, and I don't blame them a goddamn bit. If the tables were reversed and I were in their shoes, I would be thinking the same thing.

"Let me assure you, your family was only brought here to protect them. I gave that order to ensure Serena and her family are safe because Mancini does not play one for one. No, he does not want to kill me for outing him. He wants to see the woman I love tortured beyond belief right in front of my eyes. Only when this occurs will he feel redeemed. I did not have your families brought to our estate for any other reason than to keep them safe, knowing they could be used as pawns in his deadly game. I didn't know at the time that Serena would be leaving."

"Where is our sister?" Anzio shouts.

"She is safe, you have to trust me on this, and your families will be safeguarded. You also must know that she may never choose to return to me, and if that is her choice, she will need to disappear."

Chapter 12

Serena

It has turned dusk by the time I venture downstairs to see if I can scrounge a little something to eat. I know that Mrs. Caruso will have a large dinner served later in the night, but I haven't had anything to eat at all, and I am ravenous. I enter the kitchen, and it's empty, so I peek in the refrigerator to scour my options.

"Let me make you something to eat," Mrs. Caruso says, coming into the kitchen behind me.

"That would be wonderful. I'm absolutely starving. Would you happen to have some wine? I'll pay you for a bottle, or perhaps two?" I tell her.

"Sit, let me make you something, and we will share a bottle," Mrs. Caruso says, pulling out leftovers from lunch. She bustles about the kitchen, heating the leftover ravioli, and then she adds garnishes to the plate before she hands it to me.

I take a bite and then another. "So good; this is absolutely scrumptious," I say, inhaling the oregano and garlic aroma before taking another bite.

She opens the pizza oven and pulls out a wrapped packet of garlic bread. It smells delicious, and I unwrap it and devour one of the pieces before I've finished placing the rest of them on the serving plate.

Her brows furrow with concern. "When did you eat last?" she asks while pouring me a glass of wine.

Mrs. Caruso has always seen more than she should, and I don't want her to get involved any more than she is with me, because I don't know what impact that could have on her and her home. "Way too long ago! No breakfast, no lunch, and this food is absolutely scrumptious!"

"Eat up. There's more in the refrigerator, and the others will be down later for supper. You can join us then too, if you like."

I shake my head no as I inhale the meal she's given me. I appreciate the thought, but I don't feel like company, and as if sensing that, she nods. "There is a small refrigerator in each room. I'll have a plate sent up that you can keep for when you're hungry again, along with a bottle of wine for the night."

"Thank you so very much," I say, hugging her tight after I finish eating. "Do you mind if I take this bottle with me? Feel free to charge me," I say, fingering the chilled red that's sitting next to the refrigerator.

"Consider it yours, Serena, and dear, is there anything that I can do for you? Our families have known each other for a very long time. You can trust me," Mrs. Caruso says.

I nod because I know she must be wondering why I'm acting so strange. "Don't worry; I will be okay. I just needed a place where I could reflect on life a little bit, you know?"

She nods and pulls me in for a hug. "If you need anything, just let me know, anytime of the day or night. Feel free to help yourself to food or drink if I'm not awake."

I nod, trying and succeeding in keeping the tears at bay, before taking a glass and the bottle of wine back upstairs to my room. I freshen up at the sink and head to the balcony as the darkness enfolds the city lights all around me.

It is just about the same time that I usually call Nonna when I'm traveling, so I pour myself a glass of wine and connect with her number. In a matter of moments, she answers, and just the sound of her voice manages to bring me comfort. "Nonna, it's me, Serena."

"Thank God you are okay. Serena, where are you? Your brothers are here, and Giovanni has had their families brought to the estate. They tell me that you left on your own. Why, tell me, why?"

"Nonna, I just need to deal with some things, nothing more. How are you feeling?" I ask, hoping to get her to talk about something else, but she is not dissuaded so easily.

"Serena, I may be old, but I am not senile. Tell me what I ask! Where are you, and why did you leave? Did Giovanni bring your brothers' families here to get you to come back to him? Is he blackmailing you?"

"Nonna, you always think the worst of Giovanni. I left because I need time to think about some things and our relationship. He had already talked to me about bringing the entire family to his estate to keep them safeguarded. I have no doubt that's exactly what he's doing; nothing more and nothing less."

"I want you home, Serena. Whatever is happening, come home to me. Your brothers are here, and Giovanni is here; come home so they can protect you."

"Nonna, I am safe. I promise you; I am fine. I just need a couple days to reflect," I say, not telling her there's no way possible to move her or any of my family from the Larussio estate without calling attention to them and potentially putting them on Mancini's radar. They may not like where they are, but they are safe, and I silently thank Giovanni and Salvatore for this.

"I will give you a few days, but then you tell me the truth; you tell me why Giovanni ordered our family to his estate. If the Larussios have taken my family to get you to stay with Giovanni, I will have your brothers hire someone to cut off his balls!" Nonna says.

"It's not that way, Nonna," I reply, sipping on my wine, and watching the darkness take over the landscape until I am unable to see anything of the sea and only the city lights below.

"Tell me how it is then, Serena."

"Giovanni is protecting us, Nonna. He brought the women and

children to his estate to keep them safe. Giovanni's enemies are trying to get to me, but I am well protected. They will try to use our family as leverage to draw me out. I need you to understand this, to make my brothers grasp that the entire family is safe if they stay at Giovanni's estate."

There is a long pause as she digests this information. "When will you be home then?"

"I just need a couple days, then I will return." I am trying my best to get past the scene in my head where Giovanni orders innocent women to strip and men to search the most private parts of their bodies. That vision, though, the one that I've solidified in my mind, won't seem to go away, try as I will to make it do just that.

"A couple days, that is all. I will let your brothers know, and you will not disappoint me, Serena," Nonna says.

"I will see you soon. Tell the family that I am safe, kiss them for me, and let them know what I have told you. Most of all, do not worry about me. I am perfectly fine."

"I will expect to see you in a couple days," Nonna says before disconnecting, leaving me with my thoughts as the sky grows darker. I am about to pour another glass of wine when a message from Jay hits my cell.

Mancini's men have found you. Stay put! We are coming for you.

No! The last time they came for me, they blew up Nonna's house. I can't risk that they will blow up Mrs. Caruso, her guests, and her beloved bed and breakfast.

I hit Jay's phone number to connect with him. "I'm leaving, heading down the stairs, and will come out by the back porch. Make sure Mancini's men come after me and don't try to blow up the house."

I slide into my sandals and don't wait for an answer as I throw my purse over my shoulder, race down the stairs, and push the back door open. I don't see the security team, but waiting is not an option. I need to get far, far away from this house, or Mancini's men will blow it up with everyone in it. I've almost made it to the parking garage when strong hands grasp me, cover my mouth, and drag me to an awaiting vehicle.

I should be afraid, very afraid, but all I feel is an intense calm settling over me as I slowly stop struggling and wait for the very moment I know will eventually come.

When my attacker adjusts to get a better grip, he gives me the perfect opportunity. I twist, and his body is so close to mine, I couldn't miss my target if I tried, and I don't. The joint of my knee connects soundly at the base of his scrotum, and when he groans in agony, his hold on me loosens as he reaches for his crotch, and I don't waste that opportunity either. I grab the hair on both sides of his head and bring him down hard, ensuring my knee connects with the bony part of his nose, breaking it soundly and lodging what's left so deep that only a surgeon will be able to remove it.

I spin, taking off for the garage, but large hands encircle my neck, almost lifting my feet from the ground, and drawing the breath from my lungs with their force. "Not so fast. You're heading in the wrong direction, sweetheart," a deep voice growls, sending shivers of fear down my spine as he squeezes my neck even tighter between the palms of his rough, mammoth hands.

I swallow down the rising anxiety, because now it's mind over matter. He may have my throat in a vise, but he's not squeezing so hard that I can't breathe. He's just trying to scare me because they want me alive, and I fully intend to use that knowledge to my advantage.

I will my body to relax, taking breaths and drawing them deep into my lungs, fueling them for the time when I will need to run. "That's a good girl," my captor says once I've stilled completely. He lessens his grip around my neck, and his hands release their hold and trail down to capture my wrists, but I can't allow him to take my hands out of play or he will have an even greater advantage. I draw another large breath and drop my head, giving myself the distance and momentum I need before throwing it back with all the force I can muster and connecting with his face.

"Bitch!"

It gives me just the diversion I need to spin and drive the heel of my foot right into his crotch, bringing the giant of a man to his knees in agony, before I send my foot smashing into his face.

My first instinct is to run, run as fast as I can and get to the safety of the car, but I don't have that chance as the cold steel barrel of a gun slides along the base of my neck. "It's over, sweetheart," a voice says in my ear, his mammoth body dwarfing mine in height and width.

I swallow down my anxiety because there is no time for it here. "You don't scare me! Mancini's in prison, so he can't come for me himself. He sends someone who can't even fight like a man but needs a gun to keep a woman in place to do his dirty work," I taunt, feeling his body tense in anger at my words.

"Quiet, bitch!" he says.

I swallow hard, clearing my mind of anything but the task at hand, and recalling the lesson of my life: *Never use a weapon when your hand will do. Save the weapon for when you need it.* I have almost reached the one that could save my life while he's been focused on my taunts.

"Who's going to make me?" I yell, getting louder, so loud that I know he'll need to clamp his free hand over my mouth, and as soon as he moves the arm that's been close to my side, I pull the gun from the purse hanging at my waist, twist, and take aim at the only thing within my reach, the width of his middle, sending two succinct shots right through his bulky body.

He screams, releasing his hold on me, and I turn to finish him off, but a shot rings out through the night and perfectly delivered bullet straight to his forehead. I watch as the man falls in front of me, and the security team surrounds me.

"Call in a cleanup crew, and get Serena secured," someone yells.

"Roger that!"

And with that, a black sedan comes barreling out of nowhere and screeches to a halt beside us, and I am lifted off my feet and thrown into the back seat of the vehicle.

"We have heat coming in from all directions. Drive, drive, drive!"

Chapter 13

Gio

Serena's brothers are irate, firing questions faster than I can answer about where she is and why she left without a word to them. I don't blame them. If she were my sister and dating the likes of someone like me, they'd already be dead for putting her life in danger.

Salvatore has had it with the chaos. "Enough! You're not going to get answers until everyone calms the fuck down." He says it in an outwardly calm voice, but I see the smoldering in his eyes. He's clearly had enough for one day having to run interference not only between me, Great-Uncle, and the cousins, but now with Serena's family too.

"You want us to calm down, then you tell us where our sister is! We need to go get her! We will join forces, do it together; whatever it is, we will do it!" Aramis says.

I nod, gesturing at Sal to hold him at bay because I'd be out of my mind too if my family had just been brought to the estate of a Mafia family who has terrorized their sister for years and then learned that she is missing.

"Serena is safe, you have my word. She went to Naples. She needed time for herself to think about a few things, and I hope that she will return soon," I say, hoping that she does that very thing.

Aramis is not easily pacified and narrows his dark eyes at me. "Tell me what you plan to do with our family," he says.

"Keep them and you safe. I promised Serena I would safeguard her family, and that is what I'm doing. I didn't know she was going to run off," I say.

"If she ran, she had good reason! What did you Larussios do to her?"

Salvatore's eyes darken. He's reached the end of his rope at the very same time as me.

I resign myself to the fact that her family may never accept me, and they aren't too far off from the truth. "I'm sure Serena had good reason. Until she returns, I promised to keep you and your families safe, but while you are under the Larussio roof, you will not disrespect my family," I growl, earning me a nod of approval from Salvatore.

Aramis contemplates this and then nods, one curt gesture, but the message is clear. He starts to say something, but I raise my hand to wave him silent as I answer an incoming call from Jay. "Gio here."

"Mancini's men know where Serena is. We have her covered and are going in, but you have to know this could get volatile really fast. Can we depend on your men in Naples to help?"

"We have soldiers all over the city. Tell me what you need, and it will be done," I say, ignoring the curious stares and irate glares from her brothers.

Salvatore needs no further information than what he hears before pounding out a message to give our crews instruction. I see the group message as it comes across my phone screen and nod my appreciation to my intense cousin while continuing to listen to Jay.

"We will have the city canvassed. Give us the details," I order, placing the phone on speaker. Salvatore's eyes widen with disbelief. I know what he's thinking—the protocols—but I don't fucking care. Her brothers need to know what's happening and that our family is doing everything we can to protect her. And at the end of the day, we may need their help.

"We have her! She tore out of the house before we could secure the perimeter and fought the fucking men off herself. Who the hell taught her how to fight like that? She's seriously good. Serena almost took two men out and was about to kill a third one when we took the liberty ourselves. She's a little scared and thoroughly pissed off right now, but she's safe in the back seat of our car. The men were able to get a bug placed on one of Mancini's vehicles, so we have eyes and ears all over the crew right now. They're following us, and the DMV feed just popped up with a search on the plates on this vehicle, so they're plenty connected. They won't come up with anything that leads them back to you or your family."

I nod, taking it all in, unable to speak past the lump of fear in my throat for a moment. Serena is in the middle of the worst war that I could imagine and had to fight off grown men who sought to harm her. "Salvatore has every goddamn soldier we have in the area pulled off their duties and at your disposal. Lock down the entire city if need be, but you keep her safe, capiche?"

"Roger that, Gio. Roger that. We have heat. Gotta go, but will keep in touch," Jay says, and every single one of her brothers raise their eyes and shoot out of their chairs at the very same time. Nate and the other members of the security team watch them warily, ready at a moment's notice to deal with an all and all fallout.

"Get us there, all of us," Aramis says, gesturing to himself and his brothers. "We will go in too. We grew up in Naples, and we will help!" he yells, and his brothers all nod their agreement. I once thought Serena's brothers were no good, not coming to her rescue when she was being blackmailed for money, but they care deeply; they just didn't realize the suffering she was enduring. My dark-haired beauty hid it so well from them, wanting to protect her brothers and their families. They live with the guilt of not helping her all those years when members of my family were extorting money from her and her nonna, leaving them with barely enough to put food on the table, and I know they will do anything in their power to help her now.

I nod to Salvatore, conveying my wishes, and he takes in the somber faces of the men and nods his agreement.

"We'll have one of the security teams fly you in," I say after reading another of his messages out to our teams. "It won't take long by air, and Salvatore is having the plane readied as we speak. Your families will remain here, they will be safeguarded, and I will be coming with you." I glance up just as the irate glare of my great-uncle faces me from the doorway of the dining room.

"Giovanni, there's been no clearance for this! We can take care of this without all of this assistance," Great-Uncle roars.

"There's no time to waste on protocol. Her brothers want to help, and they're coming with me and Salvatore," I say.

Great-Uncle's mouth tightens, but he remains silent, glancing from me to Salvatore for confirmation we're both in agreement, needing no further explanation than that, and then he looks to Serena's brothers, one at a time, and then turns to security. "Ready the plane."

Salvatore and I probably look like mirror fucking images, shocked beyond words. Great-Uncle doesn't stray from the family protocols for any reason, but it's clear that he has become very attached to Serena.

I hit Jay's cell while Salvatore sends instruction to our men. "We need more men in Naples as quickly as you can. Salvatore is going to text you the contacts we already have on the ground in the city, along with the safe house address.

"Roger that," Jay says.

I turn away from the family and their prying eyes to walk outside on the balcony to talk in private. "How is Serena? Has she calmed down?"

"I'm not going to lie to you. She's worried about the bed and breakfast and the people she was staying with. We've reassured her they were not harmed, and aside from that she seems relatively calm after a fight for her life. I couldn't say much on the phone before, but she overpowered two of the men, and one will need surgery. Then she put two bullets into another and would have ended him if we hadn't stepped in."

My chest should swell with pride for the impressive way she handled the situation, but instead it tightens, knowing that she had to use those skills to save her life. It does not matter to me that she put herself in this position by leaving; she should have the freedom to come and go as she pleases without people trying to do her harm, without her needing to defend herself, or for a team of security to protect her.

"We're taking her to your safe house, and we have word that your men are already there to help us safeguard the perimeter. One thing you should know, though, Gio," Jay says.

"Tell me," I say as Great-Uncle and Salvatore join me on the balcony.

"We just got radio action and confirmed the instructions aren't coming solely from Mancini. Someone's calling the orders from higher up. Our suspicions were correct. He's just a puppet, and whoever's at the top sure as hell knows what they're doing. They've scrambled all the inbound and outbound communications, but they weren't good enough for our intel team. We have a lock on the airwaves, and we're very close to homing in on where the orders are coming from," Jay says.

Great-Uncle looks to me and then to Salvatore. "I'm coming with you!" he says.

"There's no reason to do that. We have an entire security team and every soldier in the city on standby," Salvatore says.

"There's much you don't know." He points inside at each of the brothers and bellows at them, "You have not yet been cleared by the family. You will know what you are getting yourselves into before we board the plane! Giovanni, Salvatore, I expect they go in with eyes wide open and an allegiance to this family!"

"It will be done," Salvatore says.

"Then get us to the private airstrip. We can talk on the way," he roars.

Chapter 14

Serena

I find myself lying on the floor of a car with a blanket thrown over me. The vehicle moves slowly at first, but I can tell when he hits the main street because he accelerates. I have lived in this neighborhood all my life, and I know exactly where we are as we stop at a light. My pulse beats faster until the car begins moving forward again. I try to lift my head up, but a firm hand on the back of my neck keeps me from raising up or being able to see my surroundings.

"Stay down, Serena. We have heat all around us, all looking for you," a deep voice that I recognize as one of Giovanni's security team says.

"Nick?" I ask.

"Yeah, that's right, but only because Giovanni had us tailing you. If he hadn't done that, you'd be in the car trunk of one of Mancini's goons right about now, gagged and driving to a place where they would torture you for hours, days, fuck—they could draw it out for weeks. Do you know what these men want to do to you to get back at Giovanni? He had you and your family safe, and you took off! I'm too fucking busy right now, but at some point, you're going to have to explain that move to me!" Nick growls.

"I'm sorry! And by the way, I was holding my own just fine!"

"I'll ease up, but you stay right the hell where you are. If you raise your head, my hand goes back on your head. This discomfort is of your own doing and nothing compared to what they had in store for you if they had taken you," Nick says. "I'm going to cover you with a protective covering. It's heavier than the blanket. Don't move, just stay under it, and we'll get you out of here, okay?"

I don't say a word as a heavy tarp-like blanket is laid over me. I've messed up badly, but I don't know how to reconcile my feelings anymore. I feel completely lost and torn between my values, my family's warnings, and my love for Giovanni. My nonna won't ever accept Giovanni. He orders horrific acts to be done, not only him but his family. How would anyone react to that knowledge being shown to you firsthand?

"Nick, we have Antonio on the line. He wants us to put him on speaker for Serena," someone says from the front seat.

"Do it," Nick says.

"Serena, this is Antonio. Listen to me. I'm sure you're scared out of your mind right now, but these men are going to take care of you until we get you back to safety, okay?"

I start to lift my head up, and Nick places his hand gently on the back of my nape, reminding me of the danger. "Lift up enough to speak, but that's all. There's extra bullet proofing along the bottom of the car. Just taking precautions, Serena," Nick says, and I try hard not to think of a scenario where bullets come flying at the car, taking everyone out except me because I've been safeguarded on the floor.

"Antonio, where is Giovanni?"

"He's on his way to you, Serena. I have the safe house set up, and it won't be long before you're safe, okay?"

I nod, more to myself than to anyone else because I know Antonio can't see me. I'm comforted that Giovanni will be there. What does that mean? Have I heard and seen too much? Asked too much? "When will I see Giovanni?"

"Soon, Serena, very soon, but you have to listen to Nick and the other men. They will take care of you, but you have to do as they ask," Antonio says.

"I will if you promise me one thing."

He chuckles loudly, and the sound reverberates through the speaker and around the car. "You're in no position to negotiate anything, Serena, but what is it?" Antonio says.

"Can you call Gracie and tell her that you're okay? She was asking Nonna about you. I think she was a little worried about you," I say.

He doesn't respond right away. When he finally replies, it's not with the answer I had hoped for. "You can let her know, Serena, and give her my best regards."

I make a mental note to talk to him privately. I shouldn't have asked him in front of the other men, or let on that I know something is going on between the two of them. I should apologize, but I don't have the chance before he starts yelling overhead. "Get your foot on the gas! We have heat coming at us from all directions! Nick, keep Serena on the floor! Don't let her head come up for any reason!" Antonio yells, and Nick's heavy hand pushes me into the floorboard even harder.

The car accelerates faster and faster before swerving. I feel my body forced against the seat, almost sucked in as we fly down the highway. "Get to the safe house as quick as you can. Scottie's bringing in overhead cover, but we need to get there fast!" Jay instructs, coming over the speaker now too.

"Roger that! I have my foot on the floor!"

We hit a round of curves, and my belly flips as the car moves side to side, hugging the highway as it navigates the curvy terrain. "You're almost to a turnoff; as soon as you see it, bank hard right," Jay yells from the overhead system.

"Roger that," the driver says, seemingly calm just before he swerves hard, and I'm thrown against Nick's legs.

"Stay on the floor, Serena," Nick says, and then all hell breaks loose. Firepower opens up all around us, coming from everywhere. "Get us the hell out of here," Nick yells to the driver.

"Roger, that! The turnoff's coming in less than two minutes. When I hit the brake, we're going to bank hard right again. Here we go; on one and two and hang tight," the driver yells just before the car swerves and fishtails, righting itself before the driver hits the gas, and we propel forward at an increasingly rapid speed.

There's an explosion, and then Jay's voice comes over the speaker. "The threat has been taken out for now. Get her to the safe house, and we'll meet her there."

The family is coming for me. The same people that I pushed away, shunned because of their tactics, the very tactics that just saved my life, have killed the men who are trying to abduct me, and they've done it time and time again. The tears are uncontrollable, and I don't even try to stop them because whatever I've felt, whatever I've kept repressed, is finally coming full circle. Giovanni has ordered people killed in retribution for what my nonna and I have endured. He had Sal teach me self-defense and has also gone against his great-uncle, whose protocols are everything. His men have now killed people who are trying to do me harm, some of the same people that I asked Great-Uncle to remove.

I didn't know it was against a protocol to ask him to help me. I thought it was asking him a favor that he would easily be able to accommodate. Instead, it put Great-Uncle into a position where he had to make a choice. Stick to his protocols, or break them for a person who admittedly had issues with the family after having been blackmailed by them for years. Great-Uncle stuck with his protocols but allowed Giovanni to go easy on me, and eventually he did call the horrible protocol off. Giovanni has been honorable, and all I can think about is how stupid I've been and how much I want to see him.

The next half hour feels more like hours as we wind through back roads and gravel before the car eventually stops.

"Heavy cover during transport. The house has been cleared, and we have reinforcements, both aerial and on the ground, but we don't take any chances with Serena," Nick says to the crew before uncovering a piece of the protective blanketing to speak with me. "Sit up, and I'm going to throw this blanket over you while I carry you in."

I can only nod, too emotionally exhausted and nervous about what has transpired, and what is about to occur, to do anything but that. Nick keeps me completely covered, and only when he puts me on the floor and removes the heavy blanket do my eyes begin to take in the room we are standing in.

"You'll be safe here until the family arrives," Nick says to me, and then he takes his cell phone from his pocket and answers with one word. "Nick."

He looks at me, his eyes never wavering. "She's shaken up a bit but otherwise fine. I'll tell her," he says, sliding his phone into his pocket. "The family just touched down; they'll be escorted in from the helipad. You should know that your brothers are with them."

After a few short moments, there's talking outside the cabin. The large door is opened from the outside, and Giovanni fills the space of the door frame, his eyes tracking me as he stalks into the room, followed by an entourage of his family, my brothers, and more bodyguards right behind him.

His eyes are dark and hooded as he takes me in. "Come with me, Serena."

Chapter 15

Gio

This fucking jet can't go any faster, and then security transfers us to the helicopter after we finally land. I just need to feel her breathing in my arms, so I feel her heart beating against my own, and it feels like it's taking forever.

We land on the helipad, and the guards surround us and help us to the ground, assisting us into the armored car that will take us to the safe house hidden deep in the valley. Every precaution has been made because I ordered it, but that doesn't put my mind at ease. It won't settle until I have my dark-haired beauty in my arms again.

When I walk through the door of the immense cabin, the emotion in her eyes looks like half relief and half fear of my fucking family. All she knows is that our enemies are after her, me and my family have found her, and that we have her brothers.

The look on her face absolutely slays me. All I want to do is pull her to me and keep her protected, but she asked for space, even put her family and mine at risk to get separation from me. Serena is tense, completely overwhelmed by everything that has happened, and the fact that not only Sal and Great-Uncle are here but her brothers as well. I want to pull her tight and hold her, explain, apologize, tell her nothing like what transpired will ever happen again, but that may not be the truth. There's a wariness about Serena, and I certainly don't want to discuss it in front of our families. I could only imagine the beating her brothers would try to give me for what I put their sister through. I can't wait one more minute to have her near me. I just need to get her away from everyone else, and I need to do it now. "Come with me, Serena."

Her brown eyes are so heavily veiled in swirling emotion that I have a hard time deciphering the storm that's churning in her beautiful depths. She lowers her eyes and holds out her hand to me.

I swallow down the lump in the back of my throat, and it takes less than three steps to close the distance between us. I scoop my dark-haired beauty into my arms and carry her through the great room to where the stairs lead to the upper level. She leans her face into my chest, her arms tighten around me, and she breathes deeply, driving me delirious with need.

I hold her tightly, but careful not to smother her with my strength. The door to the suite we will use for the duration of our stay is open, but I close it as we walk through, heading through the living area and directly to the large ornate bed that occupies the center of one wall in the bedroom.

I lay her down and remove her shoes at the very same time I toe off my own. She's still looking up at me, watching me as I shrug out of my suit jacket before sliding in next to her. "Tesoro, I need to feel your body next to mine, feel your heartbeat," I say, pulling her close and running my thumb against the side of her throat, feeling the beat, the proof that she is very much alive, and this is not a dream. "If anything would have happened to you…" I start.

Serena nuzzles into my chest, and one finger raises to touch my lips. "It didn't, Giovanni. I am okay. I don't deserve to be, after I ran off, but I'm okay," she says, lifting her face to me in invitation.

"Your request for space is officially denied, tesoro," I say before capturing her naturally red lips with my own, relishing in the feel of the minty warmth, and the fact that she is alive and breathing. I run my hands over every single pulse point she has, feeling the change as it begins to speed up, and her nipples harden against my skin. She murmurs, soft and low, a little purr, the sound that tells me her need is as great as my own.

My tongue dances with hers, exploring, as though it's our very first kiss while I strip her bare, one button at a time, until she is completely unwrapped with the exception of her lacy lilac-colored panties. "Lift," I command, and Serena obeys, shifting her hips in the air. I remove the delicate material from her skin to expose her soft, smooth mound with just a little strip of dark fuzz that teases me with its presence.

She thinks that little patch covers her from me, but she is wrong; it only entices me more. I need to taste her, to have her essence on my lips. Her eyes have glazed over, and I know she needs this too. I nudge her thighs apart, and she opens for me tentatively. My sweetheart thinks she can keep some semblance of modesty while I lick between her legs, but I won't allow it. "Open your legs wider; let me have what is mine," I instruct, enjoying the way her cheeks pinken and her eyes go hazy with lusty need.

She spreads for me, and I stroke a finger down her center, slipping it into her wet core. She moans softly as I tease, spreading her cream over the delicate folds before retracing the path with my tongue. On any other day I would make her wait, hold back her pleasure, but today it is something that I simply cannot endure. I need to feel her shake on the end of my tongue, for her to know who controls her pleasure, and who she belongs to, and to know that she is still mine.

I stroke her with my tongue and delight in her little moans. She raises her hips, but I hold her taut little belly down with my hand. She knows better and lulls her head slowly back and forth, absorbing the pleasure as she climbs. I tease her unmercifully, bringing her right to the edge before I tell her to come, and that's exactly what she does, as though her body was simply awaiting my command.

I make quick work of my clothes and pull her body forward, closer to the edge of the bed, gathering her gazelle-like legs around either shoulder as I line myself up. I watch her gorgeous eyes roll with one thrust, I sink deep into her heat and creaminess. She moans at the depth, and I hit the very end of her before pulling back and doing it again.

She moans again, this time grasping the bedsheets in her need.

I want to hear those little cries of desire and increase the pace, building us both until I am driving into her at a heated rate, over and over until I feel her pussy clench around me. Serena screams my name, clenching my forearms as her pleasure washes over her, and only then do I allow myself to come deep inside of my dark-haired beauty, the one who I will never allow to run from me again.

I stretch out on the bed, gathering her in my arms and kissing her mouth gently before pressing the beating of her heart against my own. "Do you have any idea just how worried I was about you? I pictured you taken a million times, tesoro. I know you had your reasons for leaving, but I need you to promise me that you will never do that again. You never, never leave the safety of my family or your security, capiche?"

Serena looks as though she's going to say something, and perhaps I should have approached this differently, but I don't think my heart could take her leaving again.

She snuggles into my chest deeper and looks up at me with those deep brown eyes, now hazy with the aftermath of our lovemaking, and presses a finger to my lips. "I'll never run again. I'm so sorry for the trouble I've caused, Giovanni. All the worry, all the security, and all the people who I've put at risk. I was embarrassed and upset with you. I needed a little time to think, and it's impossible to do that when you're anywhere near me. It took a little time for me to put everything into perspective. I'm so sorry, I just…"

"Shh, tesoro, I know," I say, closing off any more conversation by crushing her with my mouth. When I finish, she is breathless and quiet, just gazing at me, and now her eyes have taken on that hazy appearance for a different reason altogether.

"We will talk it through later, Serena, but for now it is enough you are alive and with me. That is all that matters right now."

She leans up on her elbow, and her forehead crinkles with concern. "My brothers, they can't be in harm's way. They have families to take care of," Serena says, and I pull her back into my arms, stroking down her cheek and then the long column of her creamy neck, attempting to calm her as I smile down at my beauty.

She's not scared that my family is here, as I had feared she would be. "They care about you, and they wouldn't be left behind when they learned you were in danger. Great-Uncle even went against his beloved protocols again to keep you safe. He called in some pretty big requests with other families to ensure the security team could get you out of that city alive. Our family will owe favors as a result, but Great-Uncle did it on his own," I tell her, pushing her dark hair from her face.

"I'm so sorry, Giovanni," Serena says, pushing up to kiss my lips.

"Tesoro, you're not near as sorry as you are going to be when I bend you over and spank your pretty little ass for your transgressions, but for now, that you are sorry is enough," I say, holding her close.

"I owe your great-uncle an apology, and Salvatore too, for asking that stupid question in the first place. If I had just kept my lips quiet, none of this would have happened!"

"You will learn. I will teach you what is acceptable and what falls outside of protocol. The family is aware of your commitment to us. If it's of any consolation, my great-uncle apologized that he asked us to hold you to the protocols, but what happened is not his fault, Serena. While our family has historically taken orders from the Don without question, you do not belong to him, and I will no longer live by those rules. I have made it clear to him that under no circumstances in the future will I take an instruction from him, or anyone else in the family, where you are concerned. You are mine, Serena, to love and to care for in all respects. I have told Great-Uncle that I am the only one, apart from yourself, who makes decisions on your behalf. The fault for what happened lies solely with me. I do not want you to blame Great-Uncle for that. I should have said no and dealt with the situation differently."

She's quiet as she absorbs what I've said and contemplates. "No, I am the one to blame. I knew there were boundaries, and I didn't think. I was angered that these men want to hurt you. Then that horrible protocol happened. I accepted that treatment because I trust you and knew you wouldn't hurt me, but I couldn't get over the fact that there have been women who had no choice, were forced to endure such a thing against their will. That is the part that hurts me, Giovanni, and they were subjected to much worse than me."

"I know it's difficult to comprehend, Serena, but every one of those women I mentioned were undercover setups. These same women you defend tried to get in bed with any number of my cousins to gain information so it could be used to harm the family. I know it seems like a horrible thing to do, and I'm not fully defending it, but in other families around the world they would have been shot, no questions asked. The women I referenced were given a chance to show their innocence, that they weren't wired." I don't tell her that every single one of them were wired, and those invasive searches were how they were found out.

"I warned you away from me in the beginning, Serena. I am not part of these activities, but my family very much is, and you know what my future holds when Great-Uncle passes. You have a right to go into a committed relationship with eyes wide open," I say, stroking her as I watch the myriad of emotions play over her beautiful features.

"I know, Giovanni, I know. My eyes are very wide open. We should get washed up and go and talk to the family. I owe them and my brothers an apology," Serena says, looking up at me.

I nod, because this she needs to do, but her eyes are not nearly wide open. She has not endured the punishment she is owed, and before I ask her to marry me, I want her to fully understand that I will care for her in every way imaginable, even when it means correcting her behavior if it threatens to put her in harm's way.

And the shower will drown out the sound of her cries.

Chapter 16

Serena

Giovanni cradles my head and kisses me gently. The water gently cascades over me as he lathers my hair, working his fingers through the long strands, massaging my nape before trailing his way to my scalp and causing goosebumps to form and my nipples to peak.

I shiver as Giovanni massages the sensitive skin in the curve of my shoulder, trailing the creamy suds over my breasts, stroking and kneading my sensitive tips with a finger and his thumb. The mixture of ache and pleasure sends a shudder of delight through my body. He draws me closer, and I can feel the hardness of his arousal pressed firmly against me.

"Feel that, tesoro. All for you. This time we go slow, but with you bent over before me while the water cascades around you," Giovanni says, turning me to lean against the stone wall of the shower.

"Hold onto the ledge," he instructs, positioning the showerhead so that it's raining down the middle of my back and cheeks as his finger follows its trail.

The heat of his touch fills me with giddy anticipation, and my center pools with need as he takes his time, exploring me with the heat of his touch.

"I like this position for a lot of things, tesoro. Perhaps this is how you receive your spanking, bent over, with your skin glistening and wet," Giovanni says.

My body heats with excitement at the dominance in his voice, and that's the very moment his hand connects with my ass cheek.

"Ouch!" I anticipate another slap to my rear and tense my body as I wait.

"Still, and do not tense, tesoro. Take the spanking you deserve," Giovanni scolds before the flat of his hand smacks the middle of my upturned ass, sending a shocking sting again, this time on the other cheek, repeating the pattern with continued swats and steadily more pressure as he goes.

It is not by any means unbearable, and not pleasurable, yet my center is starting to heat with a building pulse, causing it to warm and slicken with desire.

"I think you're warmed up enough, tesoro." His open hand fully connects with my ass cheek, and I've barely had time to comprehend what that means before he is peppering my ass with swats, rotating between cheeks and heating my ass with fire.

I try to move my hips away from the line of heat, but he places his hand on the small of my back, holding me still.

"You're doing so well. Stay in position, tesoro. Twenty more and we are finished for now," Giovanni says.

I gasp as the next one connects with the tender underside of my ass. I don't think I can endure two more, much less twenty, but he clearly hasn't heard my one-sided conversation.

"Why am I spanking you?" Giovanni demands.

"Because I put the family in a bad position and never should have asked what I did," I say.

The swat of his hand against the wetness of my ass in response not only sends a sting to my rear but sounds around the bathroom. "Try again!"

"Because I left!"

"Because you left without letting me and security know. You put your life and those who were protecting you in jeopardy, Serena."

The swats have continued to intensify, and I've lost count. I don't know how many more until we're finished, but all I can do is cry about the entire situation, the mess I've made, all the angst I've caused, and the intense pain still peppering my ass! The flood gates open, and I find myself sobbing through the last four swats.

When he is finished, he strokes my lower back and runs his fingers along the curves of my heated ass. "Stay where you are while I wash you," Giovanni says, drizzling the cold liquid onto the heated flesh along my back and ass, causing me to shiver. He strokes the soft cloth and sudsy material along my spine, rubbing gently as he soothes it over my cheeks before trailing the cloth lower and running the warmth through my folds.

I stay in position as he washes me, stroking me gently until my already aroused center can barely take it. I am embarrassed that the spanking has brought out so many feelings and aroused me to this state, but he seems to know.

"Your body is aroused," Giovanni says, continuing to caress me.

I am almost certain to come before he tells me to if he keeps this up, but he knows exactly what my body needs. He slides two fingers deep as he continues washing and stroking, and then his fingers tease, in and out, stroking along that special spot until I can barely take it. I've almost reached the point of no return, with no possible chance of holding back one second longer, but he already knows this.

"Come for me, tesoro," Giovanni commands, and the deep timber of his voice causes me to fall over the edge, shaking violently as my body trembles its release.

He strokes my spine, sending goosebumps over my skin, and then lifts me by my waist, and turns me to face him. He positions us both under the gentle spray and then gently wipes the remaining tears.

"I'm so sorry for all the pain, all the worry, for everything!" I say, and I start to say more but he quiets me with his lips, kissing me gently. "Shh … let me take care of you," Giovanni says, reaching for a soft large bath towel, drying me from head to toe, and handing me a smaller one for my hair. I wrap it while he's drying himself. When he's finished, he scoops me into his arms, takes me into the bedroom, lays me on the bed, and curls me tightly into his embrace.

"You are done apologizing to me, tesoro, but you must apologize to everyone else for the worry and the danger."

"It was selfish and foolish. I could have found a way to have time and space to think without putting myself and others in danger," I say, and the tears start again, thinking about Mrs. Caruso, who was kind enough to provide me with a place to stay, and her guests, who could have been seriously hurt. I put those people in harm's way, knew someone could have been tracking me, yet I went to stay with her anyway.

Giovanni wipes my tears, pulling me against his bare chest and beating heart. "Tesoro, all is well this time, but there can never be a next time, capiche? Our security is there for a reason."

I nod as he holds me, stroking my back, and letting his hands run through my hair for the next half hour. "Can we go downstairs now? I'd like to get this over with."

His dark brown eyes are watching me intently. "We can, but first there is something I want to ask you. Do you ever see yourself being able to get past what you now know about my family, tesoro?"

I contemplate this, but not for long. It's all I've been thinking about, what I needed to gain perspective about, with space between us and without that intense magnetic pull and attraction that seems to supersede my every thought and action whenever he is near.

"Your family is why I'm alive and Nonna and I are no longer being blackmailed."

He starts to say something. I know exactly what he's thinking and cut him off with a gentle hand to the lips. "Giovanni, it is no matter that it ended up being your cousins who were responsible. You were willing to find out who it was and take care of the situation for me and my nonna. The fact that it turned out to be your family, your own blood, and you, Sal and your other cousins stood by me and still dealt with it, speaks volumes."

His eyes darken, and his hold on me tightens as I talk.

"Even when I left and caused trouble for your entire security team, you allowed me the space I needed, when you could have had me picked up and taken back to that estate. Instead, you put security in place so I could get my head clear, spanked me for putting myself in danger, and then took care of me. I love you so much, Giovanni," I say, before kissing his lips.

His hands are quick to snake under my hair, grasping my nape. He captures my lips with his own in an aggressive kiss, exploring my depths as though we've been apart forever.

I can barely breathe until he lets me up for air, kissing my forehead, pulling me to his chest, and holding me tightly, before lifting my chin so that I am looking into his dark, stormy, and passionate eyes.

"Marry me, tesoro. You are already mine; I will never let you go, but tell me you will take my name, Serena. Let me care for you always," Giovanni says, stroking my cheek and pushing a straying strand of hair away from my eyes.

The word escapes my lips without thought or hesitation. "Yes," I say, and his lips crash down on mine. He rolls on top of me, and in one quick thrust, sinks deep inside of me, claiming what belongs only to him.

Chapter 17

Gio

One little word, yes, and the need to be joined with Serena again is primal. My cock is hard and erect, craving her heat with a need to consume her. Her pebbled nipples and hazy eyes tell me she'll be ready for me, and with one thrust I am deeply connected with my dark-haired beauty. Serena is hot, soft, and so very wet, and she moans so prettily as I sink deep. I allow time to acclimate, letting the pulse from my body throb against her special little spot before drawing out and dipping into her sumptuous heat.

Serena's light panting causes my balls to tighten and ache with need. "Wrap your legs around me, tesoro."

She does as I ask immediately, pulling me in tight, and causing me to groan with need.

I smile down at my beauty. Serena thinks I've given her a little control, but nothing could be farther from the truth. I want her in the position that will allow me to sink even deeper against that little spot, the one that drives her crazy, ensuring she is helpless to wiggle away from the pleasure. I drive deep, right to the very end of her, and she moans loudly, causing my cock to throb even harder.

"Giovanni!"

I thrust my length inside of her tight, velvety folds, over and over again, sliding through her heated center, watching her build while her little moans begin filling the air. When she reaches the point of no return, I drive hard and deep. Serena screams my name as she comes, trembling and squeezing my cock with her heated center, bringing me over the edge and spilling strand after strand of seed deep inside of her.

I rest my forehead on hers, keeping the weight of my body on my elbows, and smother her with kisses. "You've made me the happiest man in the world, tesoro. I love you so much."

Her beautiful doe-like eyes fill with tears as I watch. I scowl and wipe them with my finger. "Tesoro?"

"I love you too, more than I even know how to express, Giovanni."

I kiss her again, claiming her lips and tasting her tears as they continue to fall. "The tears, tell me why. Why all the tears, tesoro?" I demand, wiping them as she continues looking at me through the glassy film of her emotion.

"I just wish my family would accept your family," Serena says.

I push the hair from her face and wipe the straggling tears. "Aside from wanting to keep your entire family safeguarded, one of the reasons for bringing Nonna to my estate was to spend more time with her. It is my hope that seeing you happy and getting to know us better will help her accept me and my family over time. We will return to my estate and continue to build our relationship with your family. Surely she will soften when she learns that we are to be married. We will go slow with her; I know how much she means to you, tesoro."

She nods, and more tears fall as she hugs me tight. "I love you so much. I don't know what I've ever done in the world to deserve you, but I will never ever take you for granted, and I will never leave you," Serena vows, kissing my lips.

I don't know how this woman has become my world, but everything stops for her. The multitude of business deals and adventures, all of that, even the Larussio legacy, is nothing if I don't have her. "You are mine. I will come after you, and next time you won't get off with the light little spanking that I gave you," I growl, turning her to swat her on the backside.

Her mouth opens wide. "That wasn't light at all; my cheeks are still stinging," Serena says, pouting up at me.

I laugh with delight. "Tesoro, those were love spanks, when what you really deserved was a punishment. That stinging feeling is just letting you know I've been there and reminding you not to do that again," I say, kissing her pouty lips.

"Hmm!" she huffs, sliding out of bed and walking beautifully nude to the full-length mirror. I sit up, admiring the gentle sway of her ass as she walks to the other side of the room. She spins and glances back at the mirror, giving me a beautiful view of her long, curvy body, beautifully full breasts, erect nipples, and the tight little waist and belly that trail down to the dark little strip of fuzz that she thinks keeps me from seeing all of her.

She turns back to look at me. "Well, I guess it's not as red as I thought," Serena concedes.

I laugh because it's just barely a nice shade of pink, and it will be gone within the hour. "Go and wash up. We need to get downstairs before they send a search party for us!" I tell her, and she sticks out her lip but does as I ask, heading to the bathroom.

I take a moment to lean back in bed and let myself soak in the events of the day. I am engaged to the woman I love, the most beautiful woman I've ever seen, both inside and out, and she's going into this arrangement with her eyes wide open. She has been exposed to things that I didn't know she would be able to grasp or accept, but she has, and she still agrees to be mine in every sense of the word.

I sit up and glance at the huge wide grin spread across my face in the dresser mirror. She said yes, even with all the baggage that is my family and a sore ass, she said yes! That stupid as fuck grin staring back at me isn't going away anytime soon. I reach for my phone and send Sal a message that we'll be down shortly, and his response is almost immediate.

You might want to buy her a mouth guard!

If all of my family and hers heard us from downstairs, that won't be good for anyone, especially me if her brothers were privy to it.

Fuck! Who heard?

Couldn't hear from downstairs. I had to get a few things out of the office on the second floor. Damn, we need more soundproofing!

I have never worried about what the hell anyone else hears or thinks, but with Serena, it's different. Even the thought of Sal hearing my sweetheart moan with pleasure pisses me off. That was meant for my ears only. I make a mental note to have some of the rooms in this safe house soundproofed and to purchase a gag.

She walks into the room, and her long silky mane is brushed out, long, dark, and shiny. Her face is devoid of any makeup, and she is the most captivating woman I have ever seen. She has a towel wrapped around her body and tucked into her ample cleavage, holding it together.

I've given her clues, other instructions, but she should know, going in, I don't want her body hidden from me. "Drop the towel, Serena. I want to see all of you."

She slowly stops walking. I watch as she takes in my request, her cheeks turning an embarrassing color of pink. After what we've done in bed, and multiple other places, the fact that she still gets embarrassed by my commands of intimacy is a turn-on that will never tire. I raise my eyebrows and gesture for the towel to hit the floor with my finger, and she takes a deep breath and then swallows. I watch closely because every emotion playing over her lovely features is like an aphrodisiac to me, and the haziness in her eyes lets me know the power exchange is doing the same for her.

She lowers her eyes as she opens the towel.

She couldn't be more submissive if she tried. "Serena, look at me when you bare yourself to me," I instruct, watching as her eyes immediately find mine. This time the swirling of emotion is clear to see, pure hazy desire and lust. Exactly what I want to see when I give her sexual instruction. Her towel drops to the floor, pooling around her delicate coral-painted toes.

"Walk to me." I know we should get downstairs, but I don't give two fucks if they have to wait. Her breathing is heavy, and I tuck that knowledge away for another time. My beauty is so new to her submissive side, and the thought of teaching her all the pleasures that come with this dynamic in the future is heady.

Right now, she is going to learn what comes with the pleasure of delayed gratification and anticipation, although my cock vehemently disagrees with this thought. "Serena, put on your clothes slowly; I want to watch."

Her eyebrows crinkle, and her lips turn into a little frown, making it difficult to keep a straight face and not laugh out loud at her clear disappointment. "Do it now, Serena. I want to watch you before we need to go downstairs."

Her eyes lower, and my cock lengthens and throbs. They will both have to wait. She reaches for her clothes, which are still at the end of the bed, and picks up her lilac panties. "You won't need those, tesoro," I say, gesturing to the rest.

Her eyes narrow slightly, but she slides her skirt on first, stepping into it and shimmying it up her calves and thighs and over the curves of her hips, before reaching for her bra, which she wouldn't be putting on if we weren't going to meet the family and her blouse wasn't so thin. I watch as she covers her breasts with the lacy material before covering the rest of herself one button at a time.

"There, now, come to me and bend over," I say.

Chapter 18

Serena

I don't know why my body responds the way it does when Giovanni gives me instruction and takes charge. It simply does, and he seems to know exactly what I need at the very moment I need it. I can tell from the darkened eyes that instructing me gives him as much pleasure as I find in receiving it.

I follow his direction and lean over, tentatively, unsure what to expect, turning in front of him and bending at my waist.

"All the way down," Giovanni says, pressing his hand firmly on my lower back. "Touch your toes, tesoro. I want to examine your ass." My cheeks heat with embarrassment, and the moisture at my center beads with his command.

I bend, sliding my hands down my legs, letting my body slowly acclimate to the stretch on the way down. I feel completely exposed, because in this position he can not only see what he's asked for, but my pussy as well, and I know how wet it must still be, and now he will be able to see it too.

He runs a finger down the length of my slit, circling around my center, and dragging the moisture he's stolen from my center to paint my folds and clit. He glides his thumb over the delicate nub, and it is impossible to stay quiet.

"So sensitive already, Serena," Giovanni says, caressing me until I feel the pleasure building in waves, but he must feel it too, because he moves his finger just off the mark.

"Patience, Serena, you'll come much later tonight, but until then I want you without panties so I can bend you over throughout the night to make sure your pussy stays wet," Giovanni says, letting his finger slide in and out of me.

The fact that Giovanni wants me pantiless so he can bend me over and have his way with me at his wish might turn other women off, but it turns my center into a creamy pool of need. He removes his finger, and I feel the very real loss of his touch and heightened sense of anticipation.

"Stand and face me, Serena," Giovanni says.

I lift and turn to look into the deep dark pools of desire that are watching me intently.

"Tell me if there's anything that I asked you to do that you find uncomfortable, Serena," Giovanni says, trailing his finger along the curve of my breast and over the hardened peak of my nipple.

"No, nothing," I say, finding it difficult to say much more than that in my state of embarrassment and sexual need.

"Very good, now let's pull your skirt down so you're decent when we meet with our families. Give me a moment to get cleaned up and dressed," Giovanni says, kissing my lips. "You are perfect, tesoro. I want to spend the rest of my life making you happy," he says, and my heart tightens.

"I love you too, Giovanni, so very much," I say, snaking my hands into his hair as he kisses me.

"Why don't you use my phone and call Nonna before we go downstairs? The team has been giving her updates and have assured her you are fine, but she's upset that she hasn't had a chance to talk to you. Once we start talking with Great-Uncle and the rest of our families, we may not be able to break free until she is already asleep for the night," Giovanni says, standing up, completely comfortable with his nudeness.

I take him in with my eyes, and he smirks, kissing my lips briefly. "Later, tesoro," he says walking to the bathroom.

I curl into the reading chair in the bedroom and hit Nonna's number. She answers almost immediately, making me feel guilty that she may have been sitting there for hours waiting for my call. "Nonna, it's me, Serena. Giovanni said you may be worried about me. I'm fine, really."

"Well, you're the only one who is fine! The security team moved me over to the big house when the boys left, and the walls need a little more insulation. I've been hearing bits and pieces of your adventures all day long. Do you know how worried we were about you? Do you know the length of security measures these men put in place to keep you safe? What the hell were you thinking? What possessed you to do something so brash, so stupid? If you were here and a few years younger, I'd take you over my knee and give you a sound spanking," Nonna chastises.

I feel horrible hearing firsthand just how worried she was and all the trouble that I caused for security. "Nonna, I am so very sorry you were worried. I needed space to sort my feelings out without being in the same space with Giovanni, but I know what I did was irresponsible. If I had just asked him, he would have given it to me and kept me protected; I know that now."

"I don't think me and that man will ever become the best of friends, but I spent hours listening to him bark out commands to make sure you were okay, and the things he ordered cost millions of dollars, Serena. Helicopters, aerial surveillance, squads of elite security officers. But it wasn't the cost of all of those things; it was the sheer desperation in his voice. Serena, that man loves you with all of his heart. I didn't see that before, but I do now. I want you to be happy, and if he is what makes you happy, I will do my best to put my feelings about his family aside."

I wish that I could hug her, wrap my arms around her frail little body and feel her heartbeat, but hearing her voice will have to do until morning. "I love you, Nonna. Thank you. This is going to mean the world to Giovanni. He didn't think that you would ever accept him."

"That young man is on a short leash with me. He steps over the line one time, and I'll hire someone to cut off his balls," Nonna says, and I laugh right out loud as Giovanni comes walking out of the bathroom, dressed to the nines in a dark suit, crisp white shirt, and patterned tie.

"I'll be sure to tell him that, Nonna. Get some sleep, and please don't worry about me any more today. I'm not sure what the plan is yet, but as soon as I know I'll give you a call. I have to go now, though. My brothers are all downstairs waiting patiently for an explanation of my behavior too," I say.

"Hurry back. The ladies are anxious to have their men return."

"We'll be back as soon as we can. Enjoy a little peace and quiet until then. We'll call you as soon as we can," I reiterate, and Giovanni nods in agreement. I disconnect and hand him his phone, unable to control my happiness or the big grin on my face.

Giovanni raises his eyebrows and smiles at me. "You want to tell me about that lovely little smile, tesoro?"

"Nonna heard you ordering people around trying to find me. She said she didn't care about the money it cost you, but she could tell by your voice how much you cared. Giovanni, she gave her approval," I say, running to his arms.

He pulls me close and spins me around. "That's wonderful news. I have to admit, that's the last thing I thought would come out of that call, but I couldn't be happier. The Larussios will do everything in our power to make her comfortable and make sure she knows that you will always be safe with us. That's always been her concern, making sure that you are okay," Giovanni says, his dark eyes looking down at me.

"I know. She wants to pass knowing that I'm settled. I think she was really conflicted for a while, scared I was getting into a relationship that wouldn't be good for me."

"Oh, this relationship will be exceptionally good for you, Serena," Giovanni growls, lifting me and kissing my mouth before setting me on my feet again. "Come, I'm anxious for our families to put eyes on you. They want to make sure you are okay too."

I grasp his hand and keep him from turning. I'm not sure how to ask.

"Tesoro, what's the matter?" Giovanni asks, kissing the hand that just captured his.

"I don't know what I should say to your great-uncle. I mean, what I asked him to do, it was in the heat of the moment. I was sick of these people trying to get to you through me, trying to make you hurt, but now, after all the trouble I've caused, I'm not sure what to say that will make this situation better for any of us," I say.

"Serena, the family will come to learn of your passion as I have. It will take time. Just be honest. Great-Uncle has already acknowledged that he believed you from the start and never should have ordered the test, protocol or not. Come now; it is time to face the music? No?"

Chapter 19

Gio

I take Serena by the hand and guide her downstairs. I am not prepared for the angry eyes that glare at us as we make our way into the dining room where Salvatore and Great-Uncle are entertaining Serena's three brothers.

They are sitting around the table with drinks in hand, but as soon as they see us, her three brothers rise. Sal and the security team, who are standing at various points around the room, tense in readiness. Jesus, if I thought security used to be tight, it is nothing compared to now, but I wouldn't change a goddamn thing knowing how close Serena was to getting taken. These men have saved not only my life and my great-uncle's, but Serena's, along with the people who welcomed her into their home in Naples, while they were at it.

Her older brother is the first to speak. "Serena, what the hell were you thinking! Come here," Aramis says, pulling her into a tight hug.

She didn't know what to expect from the family, and the tenseness in her shoulders and the tightness of her jaw and mouth relax as her brother takes her in his arms. "I wasn't thinking. I'm so sorry I made such a mess for everyone," Serena says.

Great-Uncle and Salvatore watch the display of emotion as her brothers pass her around from one to the other, smothering her in brotherly affection. My great-uncle clears his throat, and all eyes turn to him. I'm not quite sure what to expect when he stands, and I don't think the security team or Salvatore do for that matter either. Her brothers have flanked her, making it clear that anything Great-Uncle has to say will be said to all, and they are in full support of Serena.

Great-Uncle makes his way toward her, coming to stand right in front of her, extending his hand to take hers. She takes a large inhalation of breath, uncertainty displayed all over her lovely face. The last time she spoke to him, she was sent to the depths of our home to get strip searched for wires. I don't blame her one bit for the fear that I see reflected in her eyes as she watches him take the hand she's reciprocated by extending.

"Serena, I owe you the gravest of apologies. I have lived by family protocols for years, and make no mistake, while they have served us well, I knew without a doubt that you were not a threat and still forced the protocol, simply for the fact of the rule. You have my deepest apologies," Great-Uncle says, and tears of relief pool in her dark eyes and spill down her lovely cheeks.

Her eyes lower for just a moment. I know she must be thinking of what happened in the lower level, and my jaw tightens with refreshed anger at myself for allowing it as I wait for her response. "I don't blame you; I shouldn't have asked such a question. It was improper and would have put us all at risk if others had overheard. I don't blame you for safeguarding the family," Serena says.

Salvatore's eyes raise in surprise. He glances at me and then back to Great-Uncle, who is most certainly taken off guard. It takes him a moment, but he finally nods, kisses her hand, and then pulls her to him and kisses first one cheek and then the other. "You are a treasure, and we are honored, Serena. While I appreciate your kindness, know that you will never be subjected to that treatment again. You have my word."

She nods, and he pulls her close to him, hugging her. Sal gives me a *what the fuck is going on* look, but I can only shrug and take in his uncharacteristic display of affection for the woman I love. Great-Uncle has gone outside of protocol, talking about things that should never be caught on mics or in front of others who don't have a level-one clearance. It's something he's never done, but that's exactly what he just did without any prompting from us.

Her brothers are taking it all in. They don't have any idea what happened to Serena, but they know something Great-Uncle did hurt their baby sister. Our security team has stepped closer, monitoring the situation, at the ready for these unpredictable brothers.

"Gentleman, we need to clear the air here," I say. "A protocol was broken that is in place to ensure the family is safeguarded. In the process of dealing with it, Serena was hurt. I will allow her to share the details with you, even though you are not cleared on every level."

Great-Uncle and Sal's eyes have both gone wide, like I've gone completely crazy, while the security team remain calm, just like they always are, waiting and watching in the event they need to intervene.

Great-Uncle clears his throat, but says nothing to supersede my instruction. I know this is difficult for him. He's gone against traditional protocols by even allowing Serena's brothers to be on the family jet, helicopter, and now in our home, but he did not anticipate me giving her free rein to divulge family business to them, and that may be overstepping the line too much.

The rest of my family and Sal are watching it play out. My cousins, other than Sal, are clearly upset with my directive. My family can keep looking at me like that all they want, but I will not allow the fault of this to only fall on the shoulders of Serena, who was not trying to do anything but prevent me and our family from being hurt.

She looks from Great-Uncle to Salvatore, to her brothers, and then to me. "Serena, this home is secure, and our security agents are sworn to secrecy. You are free to tell your brothers whatever you would like," I tell her.

She inhales deeply. "Thank you both, Great-Uncle, Giovanni. I am humbled and appreciate your willingness to overlook my inappropriate overstep, but you are the ones owed my deepest apologies. These protocols have kept your family safeguarded for years. I was, at first, admittedly shocked, and I needed some time and space to reflect. I was treated more than fairly and have the utmost respect for the protocols that have been utilized, especially in direct comparison to other families across the globe that I have researched," Serena says.

Great-Uncle and Salvatore's eyes both go wide at the same time. Her brothers are watching both of them warily, first their sister, and then Great-Uncle, unsure of what they are really talking about, but they know this could be a life or death situation in Mafia families, and they aren't wrong.

Great-Uncle is the first to speak, but does not address the protocols further. "You, young lady, will always have a special place in my heart, whatever you choose to do in the future. You and your family will always be protected, Serena."

I swallow hard. Damn, he pretty much told her that even if she walks away from the family, walks away from me, regardless of what she knows, that she is free to go and will be protected. He clearly has come to care for the woman I love.

I watch with a tightened chest. In my heart, I know she didn't agree to be my wife because she was frightened by what my family may do or say after the protocol breach, but I can't help holding my breath as she takes in what he's said. She has been given freedom to leave.

"Thank you so very much. You can't know what that means to me, Great-Uncle. I know it costs money, but do you think we can either all go back to the Larussio estate, or we can bring Nonna and her nurse here, so we can all be under one roof?"

I let out the breath that until just this very moment I didn't realize I was holding. My entire life could have changed in an instant. I could have lost the woman who has grown to mean everything to me.

"No! We don't move her anywhere until we find out why the Larussios plucked our family right out of their hiding! Tell us why our wives and children were moved to your estate. I gather that it's for their safety, and no disrespect, I appreciate your willingness to ensure all of Serena's family is protected, but the fact of the matter is that if she wasn't involved with the Larussios, her family would not need protecting! Who are these people that you are safeguarding us from; tell us! We can help!"

Serena's brother isn't going to be placated without an explanation, and while the entire Larussio family and many of the security guards know exactly what Serena meant, and why she worded it the way she did, her brothers do not.

Salvatore glances down at his phone and then starts texting. Great-Uncle and I get the message at the same time.

> Just got full clearance for her brothers.

> Thank you. Can we fix this now?

Great-Uncle watches his phone and gives me the nod: consent to address her brothers. "You have the right to know. Until a few moments ago you did not have clearance, but it has come through now."

"We do not give a goddamn about your protocols, family ties, or anything else. You have my wife and children in your estate. I don't think there's any ill intent here, but you snatched them from a place that I put them to ensure their safety," Aramis says.

Salvatore's eyes go dark, and he marches right up to Serena's older brother and grabs him by the lapel. "Listen, it's been a long day, and I've had about enough of your disrespect. Serena is safe, your family is safe, and not once have I heard a goddamn 'thank you' for all that our family and security team have done to keep it that way!"

"We had them protected!" Aramis yells.

"Get this. The safe house you placed them in is owned by a club who answers to the people looking for Serena. Do you understand? At any time, they could have swiped one of your wives and sent them back to you piece by piece until they got who they really wanted, your sister. They will do anything and everything to get to her, and the only way we can keep her protected is to ensure that anyone in her circle is safeguarded too."

I shudder at the visual this brings, but Sal only speaks the truth, and her brothers need to understand the severity too.

Aramis and Salvatore have both gone quiet, but I can see the trace of smoldering anger lingering, along with a new understanding in their eyes. Her brothers look to me and then to Serena, trying to take it all in. "We did not know. It would seem we owe you our deepest apologies and sincere gratitude for the things you have done. We would consider it a privilege to have you continue providing protection for Serena and our families. We will pay you!" Aramis says.

Salvatore is the one they're talking to, but Great-Uncle interrupts. "We will keep your family protected, and it will not be an additional cost to you or your family."

I nod in agreement. "Your family will be protected as our own. You will stay with Serena and Nonna at the estate until we have found the people responsible for this. I need to return to the States and will feel much better having the three of you there to keep Serena company while I'm gone."

Serena spins slowly on her heel, giving me the full intensity of her glare. A storm is brewing in those deep brown eyes. I prepare for the full wrath of her passion because I know what's coming, and the answer is most definitely no. She will not place herself in further danger, and that is not negotiable.

"We can talk about this a little later, Serena," I say, hoping to quiet the oncoming volcano, but it's far too late for that. As soon as her mouth opens, Salvatore's dark eyes widen with amusement, and I settle in for the tirade that erupts from my passionate dark-haired beauty.

Chapter 20

Serena

I don't think I heard him correctly at first, but no; he did just tell my brothers that he intends to go back to the United States without me. Giovanni wants to leave me confined at his estate, and he believes that he can lock me away from the world like a little princess. Well, I have already done that, and I am not doing it again!

Giovanni glances from my brothers to me, and his eyes meet mine in challenge. He is clearly serious about this plan. I know he just wants me to be safe, but no, just no! I narrow my eyes at him. "I will not be held a prisoner in that bubble of an estate! I am not going to be the good little wife kept at home while you fly around the world on your fancy jets, taking care of all your business!"

I eye the men in the room, and Salvatore has a wide grin on his face. I walk to him and point at his chest. "What, tell me what is funny, because none of this"—I gesture around us—"is funny to me! It is my life we are talking about, and I'm not going to waste it pining away for my husband, day after day, night after night! No, I will be by his side; isn't that right, Giovanni Larussio," I say, turning to find his eyes lit up with amusement too!

Gar! These men are absolutely infuriating. "You, you find this funny too! I will not back down on this. I will be where you are, not locked up like a prisoner. I won't have it!"

At that, his eyebrows raise. "Are you quite done?" Giovanni asks.

After all that, this is his only question. "No, I am most certainly not done, Giovanni Larussio. I want to be with you! Not left at home!"

"I've heard you out, and now, my fiery little beauty, you are going to remain quiet because it is my turn to talk," Giovanni says.

I huff, and he smiles widely at me, and that only infuriates me more. "Tell me what you have to say then, Giovanni! Tell me!"

"I gave you the chance to discuss this later, in private, but that time has now passed since you've made it somewhat of a family affair. I guess our security team may as well stay for the rest of the scene too," Giovanni says, earning a wide grin from Nate, who I give a quick glare of disapproval to. "What you didn't give me a chance to say before you marched head long into your lengthy tirade is that I intend to leave you with your brothers only for the next two weeks. This will give you a chance to spend time with your family and for the security team to double the manpower at The Larussio. They believe they're close to finding out who is pulling the strings. Once we have that information, we will put the danger you are now faced with behind us. You will give me two weeks, Serena. It is not negotiable; it is for your safety. I will not have my future wife lying dead at my feet before I've had a chance to marry her."

I breathe in deeply, letting his words sink in, and I can't even look up at him. Time and time again he is there for me, putting my safety first, but doesn't he know that being without him is like not living at all? Tears of embarrassment and frustration pool in my eyes.

Giovanni's eyes fill with concern, and that makes the tears fall even faster. He closes the distance between us and wipes them from my cheeks. "Gentlemen, Serena and I need time alone; excuse us." He lifts me into his arms, carrying me bride-style down the hall to a large office. He closes the door behind us and settles onto an embroidered sofa with me still cradled in his arms.

He holds me close, rubbing my back. My tears simply won't

stop, and they continue to run down my cheeks. "Tesoro, tell me what is wrong."

I shake my head and nuzzle deeper into his chest, overwhelmed with embarrassment for my actions and inability to get myself under some sort of emotional control lately. I should have known Giovanni would have a plan that would allow us to be together, but even two weeks is too long for me to contemplate right now. I don't know what has come over me... I am so needy, and emotional, and cry at the drop of a hat, and clingy and tired and ... late.

I sit up in his lap, quickly calculating days in my head. So late— over two weeks—and suddenly the realization that the tenderness in my breasts may not just be from Giovanni's firm handling of them sinks in.

He's watching me intently, wipes the remaining tears from my face, and pulls me down to kiss my lips gently. "What's the matter, tesoro? Tell me," Giovanni demands softly.

"I didn't want to be without you. It feels like forever every time we are apart. I wanted to go with you too, but now, well, things are different now; things are so different now," I say, still letting my revelation marinate.

"Serena, tell me what is different. I meant what I said; it will only be for two weeks."

I reach for his hand and place it on my lower belly. "Giovanni, I'm late. I think you are going to be a father, my love."

Giovanni's eyes light up with joy, and his hold on me tightens. "Serena, you have made me the happiest man in the world today." His lips find mine again, and he kisses them softly at first, but then with more pressure as I part for him.

Our passion ignites quickly, the need to be joined as one all-consuming. He is fully erect, and I am always wet and ready for him. He unzips, lifting me, and in one quick movement slides me on top of him. "I need to be inside of you, deeper, right now, tesoro," Giovanni growls, his hands grasping the curves of my bare ass cheeks under my skirt as he brings me down excruciatingly slow, settling me all the way down to the very end of him.

His mouth captures my moan as he lifts me, and then brings me back down, gliding me over his velvety steel hardness, over and over again. The heat is all-consuming. I won't be able to hold back if that's what he wants, if that's what he demands, because my center is already quivering with need.

Giovanni grips me tighter, bringing me down hard, time and time again, both of us consumed by our passion. "Come, tesoro," he tells me before capturing my lips and silencing my cry as the orgasm begins rocking through my entire body, wave after wave. He doesn't stop, instead continues to slide me over his body, extending my pleasure while releasing his seed deep inside of me.

When he finally slows, I sink against the strength that is Giovanni, completely spent from the events of the last few days and realization of our coming gift, feeling sated and secure in the knowledge that Giovanni will protect me and our child from whatever is looming.

Chapter 21

Gio

My dark-haired beauty is exhausted. I spend the next twenty minutes just holding Serena to me, knowing dinner will be served soon, but not wanting to let her go from my arms. The thought of her belly swollen with my child causes my chest to fill with pride, but at the same time with a dread I've never known before, and fear for Serena and the baby's safety. I caress her back and neck as she nuzzles into me. I would love nothing more than to hold her in my arms for the rest of the evening, but there is much to be done tonight.

Serena's eyes have closed, and she is half dozing. I lift her, laying her down against the softness of the couch, and leave her to go and wash in the adjoining bathroom. Her eyes open when I return and lift her skirt, watching me with sleepy interest as I run the warm cloth over her skin. As many times as I have cleaned her, Serena's cheeks still flush with embarrassment at the intimacy.

"Dinner will be served soon, and I'm sure your brothers are worried that I've carted you off and have done horrible things to you," I say.

"At least now I know why I'm constantly a babbling mess," Serena says, standing as I straighten her skirt.

"Let me get rid of this, and we'll go to dinner," I say, bringing the cloth into the bathroom.

When I turn, she's followed me and is watching me from the door. "I should make sure I don't have messed-up hair," Serena says, smiling shyly at me.

I pull her to me, kissing her lips, and straighten her long locks by running my fingers through her silky waves. "Beautiful as ever."

The men are still talking in the dining room and have opened wine before dinner. I slide out a chair for Serena, and her brother stands to pour us both a glass. "None for Serena. She'll have water; I'll get it," I say, leaving the table and coming back with a glass of water and lemon.

They're all grinning from ear to ear. We are in Italy. Our family drinks red wine before, during, and after dinner. It is a norm, unless of course you are pregnant, and while some women in this country continue to partake of a little wine throughout the course of their pregnancy, Serena will not.

She places her hand in mine underneath the table and squeezes. I glance over at her, and she mouths a *thank you* to me. Dinner is a simple linguini and clams, served by the staff that live on-site at the safe house designed to be similar to our estate. Serena takes a couple bites, and I can tell just how tired she is as she eats her meal.

When dessert is served, she starts to push it away, but I dip my spoon in her dessert and bring it to her lips, enjoying the soft blush that paints her cheeks as she takes my offering in front of our family. I take another spoonful and feed it to her, and then another. Her eyes have gone hazy. She loves it when I care for her like this. "Gentlemen, Serena has had a rather difficult day. I'll tuck her in and be down shortly," I say, not missing the smirk that Salvatore is trying to hide behind his glass of wine.

She tells everyone good night and takes the hand I offer as we make our way through to the great room and to the stairs. I don't miss the sleepy flicker of her eyes and scoop her into my arms to carry her up the stairs. By the time we've reached the door to our room, she is nuzzled into my chest and has fallen soundly asleep.

I lay Serena on the bed, making quick work of her clothing and drawing the covers over her before kissing her gently. This woman has become my everything, and now there will be a child, a little person that we created, who I will do everything in my power to protect.

Serena won't be happy that she'll be left alone at the estate for a couple weeks, but I will do everything in my power to return to her quickly.

When I reach the dining room, the men are talking amongst the men in their own circles. Her brothers are talking with one another, and my cousins are talking to each other, while the team of security men whisper amongst themselves. I sigh. It will take time for her brothers and my cousins to come together. I take a seat next to Sal, and he hands me a bottle of red, which I commence pouring into my glass. "So, when's the wedding, Daddy?" Salvatore says so that only I can hear.

I can't help the grin that spreads across my face. "As soon as it can be arranged. Small wedding, just family and friends. We won't announce it until we've found these fuckers, and by that time no one will be the wiser. We won't have the pregnancy announced for another couple weeks after the wedding," I say.

He nods. "Sounds like a good plan. You're a lucky man. She is absolutely devoted to you and will make a good mama," Salvatore says, raising his glass in a toast.

"I couldn't agree more, even if she is a handful now and then," I say, and he raises his eyebrows.

"You certainly seem happy with that charge. I can only hope to find that kind of relationship one day."

I glance up, feeling the gaze of my great-uncle upon me. He is smiling from across the table and lifts his glass in a silent salute, and I return the gesture.

Everyone's wine glass is filled, and the servers head back to the kitchen. The security team is still watching every move the brothers make, and they are looking at me like some sort of explanation is in order. I can't begrudge them for that. If she were my sister, I'd want one too. She is Catholic, and we are not married. I take a strong pull of my wine and get prepared for Serena's brothers' tirade because they are every bit as passionate about their feelings as Serena. I smile at the thought of the grandmother they get it from. Lord help me.

I pick up a fork and clink it against my glass until the chatter ceases and all eyes are on me. I owe everyone here a bit of an explanation for everything that has happened today. "Serena isn't feeling herself right now. She was being honest when she told everyone that she holds no ill will for having to deal with our family protocols, but she's also been going through emotional changes, which you saw this evening."

Her older brother's eyes narrow at me, and I raise my hand in a gesture to ward off the onslaught which undoubtedly is on the tip of his tongue.

"I asked Serena to be my wife earlier this evening, and she said yes. I intend it to be a quiet affair with just our family. She will also probably share this with you herself after we confirm it officially, but she is carrying our child." I raise my hand again, signaling silence. "Please, before anyone says anything to the contrary, let me make this perfectly clear. I asked her to marry me with no idea that she was with child. This is undoubtedly not what you wanted to hear, but I love your sister with all my heart, and I will ensure she and our child are taken care of and protected."

Her older brother hasn't stopped looking at me and nods thoughtfully after I finish speaking. "I've seen how much you have sacrificed time and time again to ensure not only that she is safe, but that her family is safe as well. I apologize for my rashness. Just know I was worried about my sister and my wife. I know what it is to care so deeply for someone you will do anything for them, and it is clear you feel that way about Serena," Aramis says, and her other two brothers nod in agreement.

The middle brother speaks up. "It's not going to be as easy to convince Nonna; she has a deep hatred for the Larussios. I don't know if anything can get through to her, Giovanni, but like my brother, I have seen how much you care for our sister and wish you both well."

Great-Uncle raises his glass. "*Salute!* We will welcome a new generation to the Larussio family!" he says, nodding in my direction.

"We most definitely will, but first we need to come together and find the fuckers who have a target on Serena's back. Nate, were you able to get a message to Jay about a meeting this evening?"

"It's all set, Gio. As soon as you're ready, we can get things started," Nate says.

I nod. "Thanks, Nate. The tech guys have installed updated communication equipment. You'll find the cabinet behind you and the others more than equipped to handle any conference call we need to have," I say.

Nate opens the mahogany cabinet, revealing a five-foot-long screen, along with top-of-the-line audio and visual equipment that isn't even on the market for anyone outside the intelligence agency, courtesy of our Prestian connections.

"Damn, our intel guys did a great job wiring this up," Nate says, smiling at the technological package unveiled to the room.

"They certainly did," I say, and he nods in agreement.

"We'll have Jay and the others on the line momentarily. There's been a lot of traffic this evening," Nate says.

"Excellent. I'm anxious to find out who's pulling Mancini's strings," I say, because whoever it is has purposely not gone after me or my family, but have been given strict orders to bring Serena in alive. It can only be for one reason, torture of the worst kind. This person, whoever it is, has a vendetta with me, that is for certain, but who? There are so many enemies of the family.

The monitor lights up, signaling the connection, and Jay and Matt, another security member, come into view and in a couple of seconds are connected to audio. "Gentlemen, we have a full agenda this evening. I'm sure Giovanni has had an opportunity to fill you in on the details, but there is much we have learned, and it's going to be a very long night," Jay says.

"Most of you know that Dominic Mancini has been the one issuing orders for Serena's abduction. We would have taken him out in a heartbeat if it had been that easy or uncomplicated, but it wasn't. We realized that someone else was pulling the strings at the top, and removing Mancini wouldn't get rid of the problem but instead eliminate our ability to find the person at the helm. We needed time to get to the source, but I'm happy to say that we did."

The entire room stills. The men stop drinking and lean forward, giving their undivided attention to the screen. Everyone around this table, for once, is focused on the same thing at the very same time, waiting for Jay to continue.

"Gentlemen, while we've found the source, we need to discuss and strategize our next steps, because unfortunately we are dealing with Alfreita's family. He may be dead, but his son is very much alive and is seeking vengeance."

Suddenly, everything comes together. I know exactly what this fucker wants, so does my great-uncle and Salvatore. Alfreita tried to overtake our territory and highjack the cargo transit between Italy and the United States. He even tried to get Chase Prestian, Katarina's husband, to let him use some of his shipping connections to get dirty, poisoned product into the United States. Chase wouldn't do it, which resulted in Alfreita attempting to set Chase up in an illegal possession and movement of product across international waters charge, among others.

I look to my uncle. I don't want to usurp him, but my heart is racing with the knowledge that we know who has their sights on Serena. If he doesn't make the call, I will.

"We take his entire fucking Family out, we do it now!" Great-Uncle roars.

Chapter 22

Serena

I rouse, stretching and slowly acclimating to the morning sun pouring into the safe house's bedroom window. I squint and pat around to find my phone and check the time. Ugh, way too early to be awake. Giovanni has been near because I can smell the scent of his skin. It's emanating all around me, even though he's no longer here.

I shower and leisurely get ready for the day, unable to get the thought that we are going to be parents out of my mind. I absently rub my hand over my belly through the skirt I've selected from the closet of clothes Giovanni had purchased for me while at his home, and smile widely at the reflection looking back at me from the mirror. I am going to be a mama.

I turn to head downstairs, and Giovanni is leaning against the doorjamb. "Where are you going, tesoro?"

I reach for his face and take him in both hands, bringing his face down to my own so I can kiss his lips. "I was headed down to the little library off the dining room to find a book before breakfast."

Giovanni watches me for a long moment. "I'll walk you and fill you in on the details from last night after you fell asleep. How are you feeling?" he asks, turning my face up to him so he can look into my eyes.

"I'm not ill, Giovanni. I feel good, a little troubled with timing. I want to be with you, so desperately want this with you, but what about the safety? What if they take me and kill our child? All the training I've undergone, it was intended to keep me safe at a moment's notice, but we never planned for a child. I don't know how to process this. How could I ever go against someone, knowing it could put our child at danger?" It's as honest as I can be. I simply do not know how to navigate this. I have done everything that I can, training day after day in case someone came for me, but being with child, that is different.

"Look at me, Serena. These men, they want you, but my family knows who they are now. The security team and intel has identified them. We know who we're after. It will soon be over, but until then, I need you and our little one safe. I know you are going to hate this, but I want you to stay at the estate for the next couple weeks while I'm in Vegas."

My heart tightens with sadness that he wants me away from him, but I see the look in his eye. He is not to be dissuaded. He strums his finger against the pulse on my neck and leans down to kiss me before whispering in my ear. "I love you, Serena. Do as I ask, tesoro. It is for your safety and the security of our child. Do not make me punish you," Giovanni says, watching me as his words and demand sink in, and everything south goes wet.

He bends to kiss my lips, capturing me with his and sliding his tongue along the seam of my lips, causing my center to moisten and lips to part for him. "Sweetheart, you are mine, and I will care for you and our child; you do not need to ever question this. The family will put an end to this; I promise you," he says, stroking my cheek and watching, waiting for an answer.

I don't know how all of this gets better, but I do know that he and his family have a great sense of family and loyalty, and although Giovanni and I are not official, I do believe he will do everything in his power to protect our little one.

"Giovanni, all the training. I won't be able to protect myself because I will put our child at risk." Tears fall because I am unable to hold them back.

He leans down and kisses me, running his hands along my body, settling under my backside, and then lifts me, pulling my body onto his own. "Wrap your legs around me, tesoro," Giovanni says, and I do as he walks me to the bed.

"I am not letting you take things in your own hands; I am not letting you put you or our child at risk; do you understand, Serena? I know you've grown up fearing the family, but this family is now yours, and we will not let any harm come to you and our child, okay?" Giovanni strokes my cheek, watching me intently with his dark eyes.

"How? How is this ever going to end? They want me, and while I have trained hard, I don't know if I can overcome men, knowing that in combat I may be putting our child at risk, Giovanni. I don't know what to do."

He adjusts me in his arms, holding me tight as he whispers in my ear. "Shh, sweetheart, your worries? They are gone! The family will take care of this. You just need to abide by the rules and instructions that I give you for a short while; okay, sweetheart?" Giovanni says, stroking my cheek and pushing my hair back against my ear as he waits for a response.

"I trust you and your family, but I don't feel safe without you, Giovanni. I want to come with you, be with you in case something happens." I know I'm asking for a lot and watch as a myriad of emotions play over his features.

I pull his face down next to mine, so close that I can feel the warmth of his breath as it caresses my skin. He groans, grasping my face and capturing my lips in a claiming kiss, and devouring me with his passion. His kiss is heated, but then he pulls back and licks my lip. "Against my better judgment, I can't deny you, sweetheart. You will come with me back to America. I will make the arrangements."

I grasp around his neck tighter, pulling him closer. "I love you so much, Giovanni. I never want to be away from you. My soul dies when I'm not with you."

He groans, placing me down on the soft linen and lifting my

skirt. "You are mine, Serena, and if you are so concerned about your safety and that of our child to the point that you want to leave your nonna and family, you will be with me when I get on that plane to America. I will deal with Great-Uncle and Salvatore," Giovanni says, as he hooks his fingers into the lacy material of my panties and commands me to lift before he drags them down my thighs and tosses them to the floor.

He undresses and crawls over top of me, caging me with his masculinity. "Do you know how crazy you make me, Serena? I want to devour every single bit of your heat. I want to lap up your sweetness until you're bucking against me and screaming my name, and then I want to drive my cock into you until you come all over me, time and time again," Giovanni says, nudging past my entrance and thrusting hard.

I don't move because I can't. He's so deep, and it's so good. He pulls out slowly, his eyes watching me intently as his head caresses and teases my entrance. "More?"

"Yes!" I start to push up to take him, but he places his palm against the span of my belly. "No, sweetheart. I'll tell you when you're ready, and it's not now." He holds me in place, rubs the hard tip of his cock along my heat as he drags my wetness from center to my clit, caressing and teasing, setting all of my senses on fire, while he continues to deny me the ability to move. "Take what I have to give you, sweetheart," Giovanni says, watching me with those dark hooded eyes, and when he's finally done teasing me, he drives hard; one thrust puts him deep inside of me, completely seated. He grasps my face between his hands and raises me to devour me with his kiss, taking my breath away as he begins to slowly but deeply thrust.

"Tell me how you like it, sweetheart; wrap your legs around me."

I don't need to be told twice, wrapping my legs around his waist as he thrusts over and over, and deeper and deeper. I am right on the edge; he reaches down and strokes my clit as he continues to power me with his thrusts, and I hear myself moaning with pleasure.

"Come for me; come for me now," Giovanni instructs, and I do exactly as he has demanded, shivering at the dominance in his voice and command he has over my entire body.

Chapter 23

Gio

I watch as Serena's eyes sparkle with mischief and absolute delight. My chest tightens knowing I need her by my side, to protect her myself, as much if not more than she needs to be with me, but how the fuck to explain this to Great-Uncle after everything that has transpired? He is going to hit the roof when he learns that Serena will be coming to America with me and Salvatore and not staying with him in Italy, along with all the other plans that Salvatore and I made well after he retired last night.

Her lips are still swollen from my kisses. I lick against the seam, exploring and teasing until she parts for me. I devour her sweetness, swallowing her moan as I pull her against me, already hard for her again, but it's not sex I really want. I need to feel her heartbeat against my chest, feel the liveliness coursing through her, because she has become my entire world, and my blood runs cold at the thought of anyone getting close enough to harm her.

It's all I've been able to think about since we learned Mancini wasn't the one calling the shots. If it had just been him, easy, we would have had him taken out by the men who are loyal to us in prison. Fortunately, our security team knew that wasn't the case, and once we received confirmation, we were able to get a well laid out plan in place. Great-Uncle initially led the meeting, pulling cousins in from all around the country, but once he went to bed, Salvatore and I worked well into the night with Jay, Matt, Nate, and Antonio to ensure all the details were in place.

As soon as our men have radio contact, they plan to draw them out of hiding, and when they do, all hell is going to rain down on the Alfreita family. If they thought they could intimidate the Larussios, try to remove me and Great-Uncle, and try to kidnap my fiancée, they are wrong, and they will learn that lesson in a very clear and meaningful way.

Only when each and every one of them is in a body bag will Serena and our child be safe. I will do everything in my power to ensure that happens quickly and with a powerful message to those who seek to bring trouble to our door in the future. Perhaps I am more of a Larussio than I knew, ever intended, or wanted to be. I pull myself out of my thoughts as she sighs into me, sated and happy that she's going to America with me.

I stroke her cheek and gently kiss her lips. "I love you so much, tesoro. Marry me here, before we leave your family, before I take you to a new land; let me make you my wife," I say, kissing her lips and pulling her body toward me.

Serena's beautiful red lips part for me and dazzle me with a bright wide smile. Her eyes mist with emotion as she pulls my face close to hers. "Giovanni Larussio, I would absolutely love that. Yes, yes, and yes!" she says, kissing my lips.

"You have made me a very happy man, tesoro. I'll get in touch with someone to help you work through the details for a quick family wedding, but right now I need to deal with a few things downstairs. You can stay here and read, go out on the balcony, do whatever pleases you," I tell her, gesturing toward the French doors that lead to the outdoor space overlooking a vast countryside beyond.

She narrows her darkened eyes at me, not fooled for a moment. "You want me to stay in our room because you and your family are going to talk about things you don't think I need to hear, don't think I have the stomach to hear. Why? Because you think I will think less of you, or Salvatore, or your great-uncle, or your cousins? No, you are doing what you must do to protect our family. I love you even more for that, Giovanni. Do you understand that I don't hold this against you, but I still want to be there?"

"Serena, you think so right now, but you have no idea the hell that we are about to unleash on the family that has threatened harm to you and our unborn child. Do not make promises you cannot keep. It is my job to protect you from everything, physical and emotional. You do not need to be a part of what will happen, nor do I want you to be. Let me do this alone, Serena. Let me keep you and our child protected from all the ugliness in the world, tesoro," I say, tilting her head so I can see her eyes.

A myriad of emotions run through her deep brown eyes, questioning, concerned, and then finally, at last, even with all the trials and issues she's had with this family, acceptance. I feel her body physically relax and completely submit to my request before I pull her close. She turns her face up for a kiss and runs the tip of her tongue over the seam of my lip, causing my dick to instantly harden. My dark-haired beauty wants to play, but unfortunately showing her who is in charge of her pleasure, since she seems to have forgotten, will need to wait.

"I love you, Giovanni. Do what is necessary to keep our family safe, with no shame, with no second-guessing how I will think of you in the future. Whatever happens, I will know that you protected your family, and I will be proud. I will love you for it, Giovanni Larussio, no matter what," Serena vows.

My chest tightens, and I swallow hard past the lump of emotion as I pull her closer and let her sweetness envelop me. In all my years as a Larussio, all the years I've fought to get away from the stigma, strived to make my own legitimate way, never once has anyone alluded to the fact that they would be proud of me for doing what the family does. It takes a moment to settle, and I keep her pressed tightly against me while it does.

I kiss her forehead, then her eyes, trailing to her nose before capturing her lips with my own. I'm not gentle, wanting to ravish her completely. The fact that she has submitted control, placed complete trust in me to take care of our family, putting all the things she has endured at the hands of my family behind her, is a gift I didn't expect to earn for a very long time, if ever.

I lift her chin to me. "Serena, I need to go downstairs and help Salvatore get everything prepared for our trip. I'll have breakfast and a book brought up for you while I work," I coax, stroking her cheek.

Serena watches me for a moment, and then a big smile spreads on her face. "Nonna needs to stay on this earth just a little bit longer; at least long enough to see her granddaughter married and to meet her great-grandchild. I think I'll give Kate, a call and see if she and her lady friends can help. We have a wedding to plan in less than two days," she says, smiling up at me.

"Yes, you do," I say, before kissing her lips and then reluctantly leaving the warmth of her mouth. "If you need anything, just let the security team know. I'll be tied up most of the day.

Her eyes cloud over for a moment, and I lift her chin. "What is it, Serena?"

"You don't think any more of your cousins are disloyal?" she asks, but I know what she's really asking is if there are any of the family that she and her family need to worry about personally.

My jaw tightens with the thought of any of my family having ever terrorized her. While I can't change the past, I can make damn sure that nothing like that ever happens to her or her family in the future and that she feels comfortable with my family. "No, tesoro, every one of my cousins has been vetted after what we learned. Taps on all communications and numerous other things you need know nothing about, but you can be assured that they are clean, or they wouldn't be coming within ten miles of you or your family. Your worries, they are over; did I not tell you that?" I ask, delighting as I watch her eyes go hazy and lusty.

While I would love nothing more than to stay here and reward her submission and her trust, there is much work to be done if we are to protect her from Alfreita and his men.

"I have to go now, tesoro. Plan our wedding. It must happen in the next two days since we leave for America first thing Monday," I

say, kissing her lips one last time before reluctantly leaving her softness to go and meet with my family.

I walk into the kitchen, and the look on my great-uncle's face
alerts me he has somehow been informed of our plan and lets me
know that all hell is about to break loose.

Chapter 24

Serena

My wedding is less than two days away. I need to get the ladies on the phone and ask if they will help organize this. Over the last few months, these women have become my lifeline while sitting and waiting for Giovanni to call or to come home to me.

Katarina has kept me the most preoccupied, because like me, she is just getting to truly know Giovanni and her entire family. Her mom left her father and the family years ago, not knowing she was pregnant with Katarina. I've listened to her stories, the ones about always dreaming of a father, and of her mother crying herself to sleep at night, pining away for the man she loved, and of the way Chase introduced her to her father after they met.

Jenny and Marenah have become close friends too. Sasha, though, has become my dearest friend, having gotten to know her and Jay and the security team on the plane. We have become close, texting and talking to each other almost every day. I love her enthusiasm and sense of adventure and will always be thankful for the way she took me under her wing when I was an airplane attendant aiding the most exclusive companies around the globe.

She made me feel comfortable, marching me right into the security room with her while she gave my old coworker, the blonde bimbo who was trying to seduce her man, a run for her money. Later, Sasha invited me to stay with her and the crew and play cards, and introduced me to her sister.

These women are my tribe, and they know the trials and tribulations of loving dominant and powerful men in this world, and hopefully they know how to plan a wedding in two days! I text them to call into the secure conference line that our men had set up for us, and wait patiently until they all dial in. When I tell them about the wedding and that I have less than a day or so to plan it, I have to hold the phone away from my ear as they shriek with enthusiasm!

"We are not missing this, not for the world. I have the next two weeks off on the ballet circuit, and will be there in hell or the high water," Sasha says, and I try to keep from laughing out loud at her language faux pas.

"I'm texting Brian right now to see if he can break away," Jenny says, and my heart swells with love for my newfound friend. I know the history between Jenny and Sasha. The fact that Sasha will be at the wedding and once dated Jenny's husband and Jenny still wants to be there for me makes me teary eyed with love and appreciation for my friends.

I know before Katarina says a word that she would want to be here, but she has to take it easy until the babies are ready since her last close call sending her to urgent care. "Kate, I know you can't fly right now, but somehow I want you to be here too. Can we do that video thing? So that you can be on a tele-monitor or something?" I ask.

"Oh my God! That would be amazing! I didn't even think of that. I was sitting over here feeling sorry for myself, and here you are thinking of different ways to do things! I'll text Chase and see if he and the guys can set something up. Seriously great idea, although I really wish I could be there in person and give you a big hug. I'm pretty sure that means you need to get married twice. Once, in Italy, and then when you get to Vegas maybe we can have you married by Elvis?"

"By whom?"

Kate laughs out loud. "Elvis, okay, you have to listen to this. It's a thing, I mean he's a thing; well, actually he's a person. Elvis Presley, you know the rock and roll legend of the sixties? Well, he is alive and well in Las Vegas, and he and many impersonators are marrying people all over the city in little white chapels. Well, I was thinking. What if you want to be married by Elvis, or anyone, for that matter? Shouldn't you be able to do that in The Larussio Resort without having to leave your high-scale resort, and shouldn't you be able to get married in the most opulent of circumstances and still be married by Elvis? No racing through the streets of Las Vegas, getting caught up in traffic jams, and no being late to your own wedding, right?" Kate asks, her wheels clearly going a mile a minute.

"I mean, the process is so smooth and efficient. These weddings are seriously scheduled every fifteen minutes. They don't allow you into the chapel until your entire wedding party has arrived, and once you're in, the wedding is provided, and then they move you and your entire party out of the little chapel to an outside area set up for pictures. This allows them to move one group outside while they're moving the next wedding party and their guests in. Talk about maximizing flow!" Katarina says.

I google Elvis weddings on my phone while she rambles about the details and try not to laugh out loud. The thought of Giovanni agreeing to this gyrating rock and roll man presiding over our wedding, instead of his family's conservative priest, is highly unlikely, but far be it for me to throw a bucket of cold water on my friend's vision for The Larussio-style wedding chapel. I can only imagine the look on Giovanni's face when she explains it to him.

"That's a wonderful idea, Kate! You could pick your wedding theme, right? Some people want to get married by a holy man, some people want to get married by a legend like Elvis, but what if you could pick anyone? What if you chose from any and every fantasy that you've ever had for your wedding and make it come true?" Sasha gushes.

"Oh, wait! You guys are going to love this," Marenah says.

Sasha pretends to groan. "Tell us; give us the details!"

"Well, you could do both traditional and not so traditional; you know, for every type of relationship."

"Go on; I'm following and taking notes," Katarina says.

"I was just thinking… You can cater to both the vanilla and BDSM world here. A wedding for some, but a collaring ceremony for others. You already have the entire resort established for the most high-end clientele. Many of these people are going to be into traditional weddings, a priest, albeit a well-known priest, but what if they want a nontraditional ceremony?" Marenah says, and I think all of us probably visualize the exquisite collar that Marenah never removes.

"You know what, you're onto something. We opened an entire lower level playroom. Why would we not think to have a collaring or wedding ceremony available for purchase, with any magistrate of their choice? I mean, this is Vegas! Marenah, if I set up a time, can you help us understand your thoughts a bit more?" Kate asks.

"I would be ecstatic to help, but let me touch base with Matt. He can help identify some people who would be able to assist far better in that area than I can. Is that okay?" Marenah asks.

"It's more than okay, but wait, the babies are really moving," Kate says as she sends us a video of her baby belly moving up and down and all over the place.

"Seriously, those babies should start behaving themselves. If you weren't so incredibly pregnant, what would be your favorite room in the lower level playroom of The Larussio? I seriously can't wait to check it out. I think Brian has one of the VIP rooms reserved for us when we arrive," Jenny says.

I take pity on Kate and jump into the conversation. "Seriously, I think the idea for The Larussio wedding themes is amazing, but Earth back to everybody—we are talking about my wedding to Giovanni, and it is less than two days away. I have absolutely no idea what to do. He said he would have someone call me about details, but I just want a small, simple wedding, and my family and friends to be with us."

"Well then, that's what you should do," Sasha says. "Marenah and I can fly in for the wedding with the guys. Matt and Jay can work from anywhere when not on assignment. We'll arrange for the live video for Kate and Chase, but first we need to know where. Do you want to get married in the church, or what?"

"Oh, ladies, you seriously need to see the Larussio estate. There is an entire chapel where the family priest comes to provide service Sunday morning. It will be perfect."

"Okay, so while everyone's been talking, I've been making a list. You get married in the church by the priest. If it's on Sunday, then nothing else is needed. Your family will already be on the estate, so Giovanni will just need to make plans for a different type of service. Sunday sounds like the day, my friend!" Kate says.

I don't tell them that it's not quite as easy as that, but instead make a mental note to ask Giovanni about persuading Great-Uncle to give the ladies security clearance for the event.

"Now, for the details. We need rings, a meal, celebratory food and drinks afterward. Tell me what you want to have for a meal and flavor of cake, first," Kate says, always the efficient, practical one of our group.

"A traditional Italian family dinner. The Larussios have the best chefs on-site. I don't even want to pick a meal—let them surprise me."

"Excellent. See, one more thing off the list. I assume you'll have them select the wines and other drinks in coordination with their food choice?" Kate says.

"Of course! I'm afraid it would be a dismal disaster if I even attempted it. As far as I'm concerned, the chef can decide on the flavor of the wedding cake too."

"Or you could just defer to your friends and order chocolate millefoglie," Kate says, and everyone chimes in with their approval for the traditional wedding cake that can be filled with a variety of flavors.

I laugh. "Did you catch that, Kate? Sounds perfect to me," I say, never one to turn down chocolate, especially when spread between the folds of a deliciously moist cake. "I can call Sal and ask him to put me in touch with a jeweler the family may use or know of. I have an idea of what I want for Giovanni, but we're talking about two days. I don't know if they'll be able to get it done so quickly."

Jenny laughs. "It's for the Larussios. They own Italy. If they have to work around the clock, they'll have whatever you need done by Sunday. Trust me! Last thing. A honeymoon!" she says, and the others join in with squeals of laughter.

"No honeymoon. We wed at the estate and then straight to The Larussio in Vegas!"

"You don't think Giovanni is going to want to spend a little intimate time with his new bride before tackling all the work here?" Kate asks.

"No, he won't negotiate with my safety. We'll have all the time in the world once the people targeting our family are dealt with, but until then, he'll want to stay at The Larussio."

"Well, I'm sure that won't be a hardship for you with all the deliciously sinful rooms in the lower level," Marenah says.

"I happen to be privy to all the amenity requests coming through this resort, and I can assure you that Giovanni has all the honeymoon arrangements at The Larussio all planned out. I seriously don't know when you'll have time to wear clothes," Kate says.

Chapter 25

Gio

I'm watching Great-Uncle's face, and the pulse in his neck is beating rapidly. "Giovanni, I know what you are contemplating. As much as I want you and Serena together, I will not have her used as a pawn to draw these men out. She has been through enough! What the hell are you thinking?" he roars, his deep brown eyes pinning me with a stare that leaves most men shaking in its wake.

"Great-Uncle, you've not heard the entire story. Please, sit; I'll get you an espresso and will share the plan. If you don't approve, of course we can shift course."

His shoulders and the tightening of his jawline slowly relax.

I prepare our drinks, handing one to him before settling into the chair across from him. "We are not intending to use Serena as a pawn to draw these fuckers out. I would never agree to that, even though that is exactly what has been leaked all over the airwaves."

His forehead crinkles in confusion, and his lips tighten. "Then what's the plan, Giovanni? I don't like anything that includes Serena in any way."

"So what are we discussing gentlemen?" Sal asks, sauntering into the kitchen and smiling widely before pouring himself an espresso and turning toward us. "Hope I'm not intruding, but I've just got off the phone with Antonio. He's been working side by side with the security team, and I'm completely impressed. As I understand it, they were able to get a communication lock on Alfreita's son and have been following all the airways. They just sent confirmation that they have a direct line set up and can listen to the orders and directions being given."

"That's great, right?" I ask, hoping this will alleviate a little of Great-Uncle's concern.

He is not to be deterred so quickly, though. "Giovanni, we need a plan to ensure Serena's safety and that of my great grandnephew. My understanding is you plan to take her out of the safety of our estate. How will we ensure her safety? I will not rest until I know this!"

Sal's lips quirk at Great-Uncle's assumption that our child will be a boy. He warned me how attached Great-Uncle had become to Serena, and I have no doubt his protectiveness will increase now that she is with child.

"We don't have everything finalized, but Serena is working on our wedding plans so that we can be married before we leave on Monday. She wants to invite her family to Sunday service in the chapel on our estate and have the wedding during normal service times. Toni has already begun making the meal preparations. He was livid that he didn't have months to prepare, but I think he settled down once we told him we would be having a very large wedding in the near future that he could use to boast all of his culinary talents."

"I don't give two fucks about the plans for the wedding while you are on the estate. We know that will be secure; only people with level one clearance will have access, and our grounds are safe. What you are not telling me, intentionally I might add, is that you are planning to take Serena and my unborn great grandnephew to the States, where we can't see the enemy coming like we do here. I need to know what the plan is, or I will forbid her journey to America!"

I love that he has come to care for Serena as I have, but right now I would settle for a little less of his interference. "You do realize there's a fifty percent chance that our child could be of the female persuasion? And the plan is to wed on Sunday, leave for America on Monday, and you must know that I have been in constant contact with Jay and Matt. The security team have everything in place and will not allow harm to come to her."

He narrows his eyes at me. "I know you think everything has been covered, but, Giovanni, this is not safe. You are giving them the window of opportunity they need."

"I've learned from you, Great-Uncle. I won't let anything happen to Serena," I say.

"You are not listening; you are not hearing a word of what I am trying to convey. You think you have a plan, but they are worthy adversaries. You have to assume they already know your plans and have a plan to outmaneuver you. Do you hear what I'm saying, Giovanni?"

"Serena is mine. The arrangements have been made. That is all we need to say or talk about!"

"I am still the head of this house and will forbid you taking her to America!" Great-Uncle roars.

I glance over at Salvatore, and his body is tense, and his eyes are dark with emotion while he contemplates the conversation. "Sal, give me your thoughts! I need her to be safe, but I need her to be with me!" I growl, running a hand through my hair.

"Just the fact that you're asking is telling. There's not one member of our crew who wouldn't lay down their life for her and the life she's carrying. I'm not convinced that we can keep her as safe outside of the estate as we can on it, but I understand your dilemma. If you keep her a prisoner, locked up at home without you, she will wither, and even though you said for two weeks, we all know this could go on much longer than that. Then what?" Salvatore says, and even though we worked through a plan we were both comfortable with last night, we are still concerned about her ultimate safety.

"Jay and his team have saved our lives time and time again! I believe they will keep her safe. Uncle Carlos has a large crew, and we will use them to keep her safeguarded while at The Larussio too," I say, avoiding the fact that Salvatore and I have already made plans to take Great-Uncle with us as well. He may be getting up there in years, but he always needs to be in the thick of things, and it is best that he is with us, for his peace of mind and for ours.

"Jay has everything under control and has been keeping me apprised. They believe they have a communication lock on Alfreita's son, but they want to make sure it's not a ploy," I say.

"If Alfreita's men are worth their salt, they knew the minute a communication lock was close and redirected it. It's not safe," Great-Uncle says, unwavering on his position.

Sal smiles widely, and his jaw shifts to the left as he glances at me. I have no idea how Great-Uncle has learned this stuff over the years, but he never ceases to amaze us with his vast knowledge of things that we pay others to do for the family.

"I'm sure the team has it well under control. If it makes you feel better, we can pull a meeting together with Jay and have him go over all the plans in detail with the three of us. If anything needs to be altered, we can do it at that time," I say, taking in the tenseness that crept back into his posture slowly starts to dissipate.

"Very well, but if I am not completely satisfied with the plans, we do not go."

I hold back a smile. No need to mention that Sal and I want him to come to the States with us. He's clearly just invited himself.

"Agreed," Salvatore and I say in unison.

"In the meantime, I need to make a few calls and some arrangements for the public grand opening of The Larussio. The VIP guest opening went extremely well, and Katarina is working on the next public grand opening. She and our marketing team want to extend an invitation for the entire city to come in and take a look, win some prizes and stuff. I think Katarina's even more excited about this than she was about the ribbon-cutting ceremony.

Great-Uncle turns his scowl back to me. "My great-niece should be resting, and you have her working on a grand opening for the entire city?"

I've managed to get on Great-Uncle's bad side, and I have no doubt I'll stay there until his concern for Serena is alleviated. Sal suppresses a smile and turns away from us, walking toward the sideboard to place his empty glass on the crystal tray that will be removed by the waitstaff later in the day. "You do know that I have absolutely zero control over what my cousin does and does not do? Perhaps you should put in a call to Chase. He's about the only one she listens to about things like this."

"I will indeed. She needs to stop working so much. All the details and all the organizing, that can lead to stress. Exactly what she is supposed to be avoiding until the babies come!"

I nod, silently agreeing with him, but I have too many other things to contemplate right now and so many things to do. "I trust you'll call Chase and see what he can do to intervene. We have plenty of people who could be taking care of all the details if she would just hand over the reins," I say, smiling to myself because I already know that's highly unlikely.

I see how Katarina drives herself and others, so much like her father, pushing until every single thing is perfect, but right now I need to deal with one thing at a time, and there is much to do in a very short time if everything is to go as planned, including getting all of us from this safe house back to the Larussio estate safely. In two days, we will be married and on a plane to Vegas to put an end to this nightmare.

Chapter 26

Serena

The dress I've chosen is neither frilly nor long, instead a short and fitted chic design with delicate straps to hold up the low-cut bodice, white in color, and adorned with simple lace gloves. I twirl in the mirror and gaze for a moment at the image staring back at me. I can barely believe that today I will become Giovanni Larussio's wife, for better or worse, in sickness and in health, until death do us part. I am also vitally aware that after this celebration, we will finally leave these walls, and with that, be giving our enemies the opportunity to snatch me or outright kill Giovanni.

I inhale deeply. This is what I want, to be free, to be by his side, regardless of the risk. I know he has only relented so that he can personally safeguard me and our child, and I can't help the nagging dash of fear that seeps in, try as I might to keep it at bay.

I instead concentrate on adjusting a wisp of hair that has fallen from the pearl slide comb the hairdresser used to sweep my hair on one side, letting the rest fall around my shoulders and down my back. I touch up my lipstick and inhale deeply. It is time.

I walk slowly down the hall to the top of the curved staircase and meet Aramis, who will give me away to a man we've always viewed as the enemy.

"You look radiant, absolutely glowing. Are you okay?" he asks, kissing both of my cheeks.

"I feel fine, really. I'm just a little nervous. It's a big day."

"I never thought I would give my only sister to a Larussio, but I've never seen a man more devoted. Giovanni loves you with all he has, and even Nonna has accepted that. She's actually sitting downstairs next to Giovanni's great-uncle. She said to keep him in line," Aramis says.

It's all I've wanted, her acceptance of the man I want to spend the rest of my life with. I thought the day would never come, but it is here, and as the organist begins piping music through the chapel and it drifts upstairs, I know in my heart that I am ready.

Aramis guides me slowly down the stairs to the great room. Everyone in the adjoining Larussio chapel is seated and turned to watch us through the large double doors that have been fully opened for the occasion. We reach the bottom and walk through the great room and into the chapel. We take the rehearsed pause as the organ grows softer, before continuing down the aisle. I can feel the heat of Giovanni's gaze burning into me, heating my skin, and searing it with his want until it reaches my face.

His dark eyes are full of emotion and mirror my own with the love reflected there, as Aramis guides me to his side. When the priest asks who gives us in marriage, I look to the family gathered, expecting my brother to respond, but to my surprise, Great-Uncle is sitting next to Nonna, assisting her with a mic she's been given, and her voice rings out clearly: "I do. Her grandmother," and the smile on her face as she gives her blessing thoroughly warms my heart.

I swallow past the lump in my throat as I say my vows, repeating after the priest, and promising to love and obey my husband until death do us part. I do not miss the importance of that promise, nor heed it lightly. When I finish, he inhales deeply, and his eyes turn dark with emotion as he repeats his vow to love and honor, and forsake all others, and to keep me in sickness and in health, until death do us part. When the priest pronounces us husband and wife, Giovanni has me in his arms and needs no instruction to kiss his bride. Cheers ignite the room, and when he lets me up for breath, his eyes are dancing with delight and devotion.

He lifts me, twirling me around before placing me on my feet again. "I love you, tesoro. You've made me the happiest man in the world. I am a husband and soon to be a papa," Giovanni says, cradling me against him before guiding me down the aisle and past our close friends and family. I blow a kiss to Nonna and Great-Uncle, and their eyes are moist with emotion.

We are greeted by photographers who move us from area to area, capturing pictures in and out of the gardens, doing their best to capture the magic of the day. When finished, Giovanni guides me inside to the receiving line, where our family and friends greet and congratulate us.

Giovanni manages to free us from our well-meaning friends and family and leads me up the curved stairs to our room. "Let me take one last look at you before I peel you out of this dress," he says, twirling me to unzip my dress before pulling me back against his hardness.

His mouth finds the soft shell of my ear and travels down my neck as he peels the dainty straps of my dress from my shoulder. His mouth captures the sensitive skin between my shoulder and neck, causing me to moan as he bares my breasts, letting the silky material of the dress fall to the floor and gathers in a pool around my high-heeled feet.

"Officially mine, tesoro," Giovanni says, picking me up and placing me on the bed while he quickly divests himself of clothes. He is built like an Adonis and completely erect, his cock is pulsing and hard with desire, but he is in no hurry, kneeling by the edge of the bed to spread my legs.

He kisses my mound, tracing around the freshly bared skin, teasing me with his breath as his hands slip beneath me. He caresses my hips and grasps my cheeks with his firm hands. He caresses me with his tongue until the desire at my center is almost too much to bear, and my hips seemingly rise of their own accord.

He nips my mound, a warning. "Still, tesoro, I will give you your pleasure," Giovanni says, dipping his tongue lower and licking right around that bundle of nerves but never touching it, teasing me until I have to grasp the coverlet in order to remain still.

"You did so well, Serena, you deserve a reward," Giovanni says, finally letting the warmth and wetness caress my swollen clit.

I moan with desire as he strokes and caresses me, over and over, softly, just a little pressure, building my desire, just teasing until I can't take it any longer.

He captures my clit with his mouth, sucking hard as I tremble around him, wave after wave spilling through me. He takes his time, capturing every drop and extending my pleasure before he stands, pushes my heeled ankles around his neck, and plunges into my wetness with one quick thrust.

My center is still pulsing and sensitive, and he drives deep, all the way to my core, hitting that special little spot that builds a different type of pleasure deep inside of me. He knows exactly what he's doing as he grasps my ass and thrusts deeper, angling himself to hit that special spot over and over, again and again.

"You're going to come again for me, tesoro," Giovanni says, knowing it's right around the corner, and then, just as the swell of pleasure is too much to hold back, he tells me to come, and my entire body trembles with obedience as he drives hard and releases deep inside of me.

He rolls me over and cradles me in his arms, pushing the hair that has managed to work its way out of the comb from my face so that he can kiss me. I love Giovanni's kisses and curl into his body's firm warmth.

"As much as I'd love nothing more than to keep you in my arms, we need to go downstairs, cut the cake, and then we need to leave," Giovanni says, kissing me gently as we recover from our lovemaking.

"I thought we were supposed to have dinner and leave after we said goodbye to everyone tomorrow."

He smiles gently, taking pity on the fact that I'm too curious not to ask these things, but he silences me with a finger to my lips. "We have multiple cars leaving for the airport. The first few will be the safest. Anyone watching will assume we would stay for the entire dinner."

I should have just let myself believe it was because he couldn't wait to have me by himself, but there is danger in leaving these walls, and he has clearly prepared in advance.

"We must take precautions, tesoro," Giovanni says, gently caressing my cheek.

"It's okay. I should have known that we wouldn't do what was planned and would be known by others. It makes complete sense. I'll jump in the shower, and then we can go eat cake, smile for more photos, and say goodbye to our family." I hurry to the bathroom, clipping my hair before turning the water on to let the stream run down my back.

I intend to quickly rinse off, but Giovanni walks into the shower and smirks at my attempted look of indignation. "This is part of the obey part. You have to do what I say, when I say," he quips.

"Oh, really! And just what is it that you want me to do right now, sir?" I ask.

His eyes light up at the salutation. "Oh, I like that very much. While there are a multitude of things I want to teach you right this very moment, time is of the essence, so raise your hands and hang onto the bar while I wash you," Giovanni instructs, soaping his hands with the creamy wash and gliding them over my skin, starting at my neck and working his way down my body. He takes time to stop at all my pleasure points, paying extra attention to getting my nipples extremely clean.

My center is aching with desire by the time he begins heading south, soaping my stomach and fingering my belly button. "All the little parts have to be clean," Giovanni says, his eyes dancing with delight as I squirm with desire. He strokes lower with soapy fingers, caressing and washing me, leaving me a puddling mess of desire before reaching for the bottle of lube on the ledge of the shower. He drizzles the clear liquid onto his fingers, all the while watching my reaction, before turning me around and guiding me into a bent position with the gentleness of his touch.

"Spread for me, tesoro," he instructs as he trails his fingers between the slope of my cheeks, spreading me until he finds the little button he's looking for.

He rubs gently, stroking the circle of muscle before sliding one finger in firmly, the tight ring giving way to his insistence before he inserts another. He crosses them, stretching the delicate tissue before removing them and gently sliding a plug into place.

"This was made especially for you, tesoro. It will allow me to control your pleasure with one click of the remote until I decide it is time to remove it," Giovanni says against the sensitive shell of my ear, causing me to shiver with uncontrolled desire.

He spins me to face him, giving my mound a quick kiss before standing up and taking the showerhead from the wall and lightly rinsing me.

"So much more I want to do with this little water wand, but we must hurry; we will finish this later," Giovanni says, kissing my lips, and silencing my moan of frustration at being left with a pulsing and needy center.

<h1 style="text-align:center">Chapter 27</h1>

<h2 style="text-align:center">Gio</h2>

The act of restraining myself from driving my cock into her sweetness again and again before we leave is pure torture, but we are on a tight timeline, and security protocols need to be followed to the letter. I turn off the water and dry my pretty and pouty wife with a soft, fluffy towel and then swat her ass playfully. "Get ready, and be quick. I'll be out in two minutes." She's finished brushing her teeth and is touching up her makeup as I get out of the shower and dry off.

Her cheeks are turning a nice color of rosy as she sneaks a look at my hardened length, and her greedy little hand reaches out to stroke me. I move in closer, unable to deny her this touch, but she strokes longer and rubs my length against the silky bareness of her freshly waxed mound. "Serena, behave yourself, and go get dressed, or we're going to miss our flight," I growl good naturedly, pulling her in for one quick kiss before reluctantly letting her go.

When we're ready, I guide her down the stairs with a possessive hand to the small of her back. We enter the great room, and it is bustling with family who are all enjoying the chef's rich hors d'oeuvres and champagne before dinner.

"While it's not tradition to cut the cake first, you all know what a sweet tooth my wife has," I tell the crowd and catch her fake glaring at me. I smirk at her; she can't deny her love for chocolate. I am so right about that.

The crowd gathers around us and the cake at the small table where it is displayed. "Please help us enjoy the memory of cutting the cake before it's time," I say, taking Serena's hand in my own as we cut the first piece of the three-tiered cake together. We each take a forkful and feed it to the other while the photographers capture the memories of our adventures, but now it's time to go.

I guide her purposefully through the throng of family and into the kitchen. Antonio and Nate are ready and bustle us to the back of the room. "Tie up your hair, put this on your head, and then the jacket," Nate instructs Serena, who quickly does as she's asked.

Nate pulls the visor a little lower on her face. "Good, you next," he says, handing me a jacket and instructing me to use the hood. "It won't look suspicious since it's just started raining like there's no tomorrow," Nate says, opening an umbrella for us as we are ushered through the back door by a team of security.

A large black Lincoln is waiting. Security holds the door open as I assist Serena in and slide in next to her. The door is quickly closed, and Nate and Antonio jump into the front seats. "All clear; let's move," Nate says.

Serena watches out the window as we drive through our property, each second getting closer to leaving the safety and security of the family estate. A part of me wants to call this off right the hell now, take her back inside, never let her out of the house or off of these grounds, to keep her protected from all the evil that I know lives beyond these walls. But I know that is not what she wants, and Sal's prediction is right. She would wither and die, so I swallow past my uneasiness as we make our way through the gates of the estate that would keep her safe, though a prisoner to its walls.

"Jay has an update. Mind if I get Sal and your great-uncle on the line and then patch it through the speakers?" Nate asks, pulling me out of my reverie.

"Do it!' I say.

"Roger that," Jay says, and I smile at the saying I've become accustomed to hearing from him and the rest of the team.

"Nate, you have me on speakerphone?" Jay asks from overhead.

"Roger that, we have everyone on the line. We're all ears," Nate says.

"Gentlemen, the team got absolute confirmation that Alfreita's son is calling the shots, and others who are involved are in the process of being identified. They tried blocking our communications lock, but our intel team is par excellence. We were able to scramble the redirects and unlock the codes. We were able to get filters in place, so they won't be able to detect we're monitoring. That's the good news, folks. The bad news is that hell is about to head into the city of Las Vegas, and they're coming in from multiple directions, and many are on two wheels.

"A dozen or so members of Alfreita Jr.'s gangs are heading into the city by way of European flights. Some of our best men are already getting into position and will have them secured before they even set foot through the airport door. The larger problem is that we have about four hundred motorcycles from a badland gang in California heading to Vegas under Mancini's direction. He's been moving product through them all over the United States."

Four hundred men, that's a lot of manpower. I try to remain calm even though the blood coursing through my veins is anything but. "How is it that Mancini wields so much control over this motorcycle club?" I ask.

"Dominic was working for Alfreita Jr. and Vicenti, who's head of the Colombian cartel. Neither knew he was working for the other, or they would have killed him before signing him on. We have confirmation that just like he did in Chicago, he's managed to embezzle millions of dollars' worth of product from Vicenti. We haven't pieced it all together just yet, but we think Alfreita Jr.'s men knew what Mancini was doing, somehow confiscated the product, and cut it with poison before it was shipped to the States. Mancini was bragging that he had top-grade Colombian product, which anyone in the field knows is the trademark for Vicenti. Alfreita Jr.'s men and Mancini make a huge monetary score, while killing Vicenti's premium product brand. Once it hits the States, most of it's running on the backs of motorcycle gangs across the United States by way of connections Mancini made in prison. The unfortunate part is it's a deadly mix, and it's heading straight for Vegas at this very moment."

Serena sits up straighter next to me. "Kate's told me all about those men! She went to see Vicenti to persuade him to help Chase when Alfreita Sr. tried to implicate Chase, but he wouldn't turn information over to Interpol because it might bring trouble to Vicenti's door, even though it proved his innocence."

Serena's eyes go wide, and she swallows hard, seemingly just realizing how much she's divulged that my dark-haired beauty should know nothing about.

I narrow my eyes at her and try to contain my smile. "You and the ladies chat about such things?" I ask.

She bites her lip, and I need no further confirmation and make a note to touch base with their husbands about their little indiscretions.

"Vicenti is known for his sharp business acumen, feared by most, but has proven himself to be a fair man. He has Chase Prestian's respect and that of his family. He was livid when he learned his product had been tampered with at that time, and I imagine he would feel the same way about it happening now. When Vicenti learns his street-grade product has been cut with poison and is floating around on the backs of a motorcycle gang that Dominic Mancini is controlling, nothing good will come of this," Jay says.

"What do you need from us?" I ask, wishing Serena were not sitting right next to me and that I could keep her sheltered from this worry.

"Given the history, we've conferred with Chase and Brian on the matter too. We'd like to reach out to Vicenti, give him an opportunity to rein Dominic in his own way. As you can understand, this would give him the opportunity to save face and meet our end goal in the process," Jay says.

I'm grateful not only for the approach in which he's handling the incredibly charged situation, but also for his choice of words when speaking of Dominic's demise in front of Serena. He and his team not only understands the immediate need for security, but the political dynamics that come with our life. I already know how I will vote, but I'm not the Don of this family, and even if I were, I'd want Sal's weigh-in too. "Great-Uncle, Sal? Your thoughts?"

"Vicenti has been wronged and will want to right this in his own way. Get him on the line. I will speak with him personally, and together we will decide how to deal with this," Great Uncle says.

"Completely agree," Sal says.

"Roger that. In the meantime, Giovanni, your jet has been cleared and has everything you've requested for the flight. Sal and your great-uncle will be arriving at the airport in about half an hour," Jay says.

"I am sincere when I tell you that your security team has become an extension of our family, and we greatly appreciate all the hard work and dedication to keeping our family safeguarded," I say, and then almost immediately receive a text from Jay.

> The order just went out to pick Serena up alive. Didn't want to share that with her in the car.

"Fuck!" It just slipped out, but Serena looks at me expectantly, waiting for me to provide an explanation for my sudden exclamation. I owe her the truth, even though I'd love more than anything to keep her blissfully unaware.

Serena manages to stay her curiosity until we've been safely transferred to the jet and are in the main cabin by ourselves. "Tell me, Giovanni," she says, looking up at me with those expressive deep brown eyes.

I wish to God that this was something I could shelter her from, but I recall Jay's warning about ensuring she knows the dangers at all times. I'm just glad he had the foresight to let me tell her in my own way. "Our intel picked up instruction from Mancini. His orders were to pick you up as quickly as possible," I say, closely watching her reaction and squeezing her hand in reassurance.

She swallows and tries to look brave, like this doesn't faze her, but I watch the storm of emotion in those deep brown eyes that belies her outward calm.

I nod, taking in her incredulous look. She has no clue how these families work, using whoever they can to get what they want. Vicenti will deal with the motorcycle gang in his own way, but it may not be soon enough if they are already on their way to Vegas. If we receive proof this motorcycle club took money to kidnap my wife and bring her to Mancini's men so they can slowly torture her, it will not be enough for Vicenti to exact his revenge. They will wish they were in hell when the Larussios finish and before Vicenti even begins, but I do not tell my dark-haired beauty this. Instead I caress her cheek. "Trust me, tesoro."

Chapter 28

Serena

Giovanni holds me close. The fact that we have a prison lord after me is bad enough, but to learn that an entire crew from Europe is being flown in and a 400-plus motorcycle gang is coming means that they are more serious than ever, and that reality is really sinking in. Motorcycle gangs are coming for me, but it's not just me anymore. We have to think about our child, and all of a sudden, I wonder if I should have just stayed in the estate and kept me and our little one safe.

Giovanni lifts my chin so that I have no choice but to look into his eyes. "Serena, I know what you're thinking; put it out of your mind. This is not your fault, not because you decided to come with me. The only reason we are in this situation is because I am a Larussio. This has nothing to do with you except that you are with me, tesoro. I told you that before, but now you see the reality. Tell me if it is too much. If it is, I will have you moved underground and given a new identity. You will be safe with our child."

Tears that I am unable to contain spill from my eyes. I grasp his face and pull him to me. "Giovanni Larussio, I know that you want me to be safe, but being without you is worse than the most horrible death. I love you, and I can't imagine a life without you that I would be happy in. I have every confidence that Great-Uncle and Vicenti will talk and come to an agreement. In the meantime, your entire security team will keep us safe, yes?"

Giovanni pulls me to him, and I don't say a word for a moment, content just to have him hold me. "They will keep you protected. We'll let Great-Uncle and Sal negotiate with Vicenti, and you won't leave security's sight, capiche?" he says.

"You told me what Mancini and his team would do with me if they kidnapped me, but will the motorcycle crew do the same, or worse?" I ask.

His eyes darken with intensity. "Serena, you will be protected, and there is much that I will not allow you to think about needlessly."

I take his face in my hands and kiss his lips. "Okay, but tell me, if they take me in Vegas, how will you find me? I want to be prepared."

Giovanni runs his hands through his hair, contemplating my question. "I'll show you, but know this, I will not apologize for doing everything within my power to keep you and our child safeguarded. You asked, you want to know, and you have that right, so I will tell you. We've installed a new app on your cell," Giovanni says, showing me the app on his phone.

This application is everything that it shouldn't be. An open window to my every private movement, a spying device so that he and his crew can track my every movement. He skims the app, and I watch myself as he does on the miniature monitor.

"Go back. How far does it go back, how much do you see, and how much do you allow your security team to see?" I demand, cringing at the thought that not only Giovanni but his entire security team has seen me at my most vulnerable, away from him and scared, in my room pleasuring myself for Giovanni. Every bit of my privacy has been a façade, instead displayed on his camera for all his team and the world to see. "How far back does it go, Giovanni?" I ask, barely above a whisper.

He drags his finger along my cheekbone and down to my lips, grazing them with the pad of his finger. "I had it installed after we thought you had been taken. Antonio and I wanted a backup, and still do, at least until this is all over. Then it can be removed, tesoro."

My chest tightens. "All this time, Giovanni. All this time that you asked me questions about my day, but you already knew the answer because you were spying on me. You were watching me on your phone, that camera thing. Who else did you let watch me, Giovanni? Tell me, did you let your security team watch my intimate moments, the moments we shared when I thought it was just you and me?" I ask, and as much as I hate it, tears stream down my face.

He strokes my cheeks and captures the tears that are now falling freely down my face. "Tesoro, you know better. How could you ever think that what we have was shared, that I would ever allow anyone to look at you the way I do, to see you in a state of passion? I would not allow it. You are mine and only mine. The cameras are for me only, to ensure that if you are ever taken, I will be able to find you, to ensure your safety; understand?" Giovanni says, wiping the tears that are still falling from my eyes.

I glance up at him, and his dark brown eyes drink me in, capturing me with all the shared emotion. "Giovanni, how do we move on, how do we become a normal family, and how do we ensure that our child is safe? Tell me, how do we do this when everyone in the world is trying to prevent that, to capture me and to destroy you?"

"We move on with your complete and absolute trust, Serena. I will never allow you to be taken, to be hurt; do you understand? This is the only reason I have the camera; it is for your protection," Giovanni says, glancing into my eyes and then down to my belly.

I want to be angry, I should be angry, but all I can feel is the sincerity of his love and possession. The love he has for me and our unborn child. I look into his eyes and stretch on tiptoes to bring his face to mine. "I love and trust you, Giovanni. Do what you must," I say, kissing his lips before his hand reaches under my hair to grasp my nape and pull me closer.

His eyes are heated and lusty as he looks down at me, searing and possessive, and his breath is so close, igniting the heat at the center of me. "Do you know what you do to me, Serena? I can't see straight for want of keeping you by my side, protected and safe," Giovanni says. His lips capture mine, his tongue stroking hot and molten across my lips until I part for him. He lifts me into his arms, and his tongue finds mine, embracing it in an erotic dance that makes my center heat and leak with desire as he carries me into the master suite of the Gulfstream.

Chapter 29

Gio

I've barely closed the door behind us when I instruct her to strip. She is the most beautiful woman I have ever seen, and I watch possessively as her deep brown eyes sparkle with flecks of gold as her gaze heats my skin. "Do it now, Serena. I want to see all of you, tesoro," I say, loosening my tie and settling into the armchair in the corner of the room as I wait for her to obey my instruction.

Her cheeks pinken, and she bites her lower lip, trying to settle her embarrassment as she balances on her heels. She starts with her blouse, the light pink gauzy material that sets off her dark hair and lips so perfectly. When she pulls it from her frame, she lets it drop to the floor and flips her hair forward. The movement shifts her hair over her breasts, and my cock hardens with desire and need, but my little submissive is trying to top from the bottom and thinks she's the one in charge. I'll let her play for a short while, and then show her who's really in control of her pleasure and what happens when she disobeys me in the future.

Her eyes dance with delight as she undoes her bra clasp before sliding one lacy strap down the length of her toned arms, glancing at me, teasing me with her show. My cock turns to steel awaiting the main reveal, enjoying the show far too much to put an end to it this soon. She glides the second strap of material down her other arm, keeping the material close while covering her breasts from me.

I wait for a few seconds, before I need her bared before me. "Let me see all of you," I growl, way more intense than intended, as my cock pushes painfully against the constraints of my dress pants and the zipper that keeps it contained.

She smiles at me, and it's clear my dark-haired beauty is having way too much fun.

"Tesoro, do not continue teasing me unless you wish to go without tonight. Perhaps I should restrain you and bring you to the brink of orgasm repeatedly, just to deny you," I say, watching as her eyes go wide with the realization of what that may be like.

Her lips turn up in a cute little pout, and her eyes flash in silent defiance, but she obeys, tossing her long, dark mane of hair behind her as she pulls the white lacy material from her body, letting it slip to the floor as she exposes her perfectly shaped breasts and dark, erect nipples to me.

I slide my hand into my pocket, hitting the button that sends a pulsing rhythm to her behind, just to let her know who's really in charge of this scene. I watch as her eyes go wide with surprise and then hazy with lust as it continues to thrum. "Remove your skirt, but leave your heels on," I instruct, because I already know that she doesn't have panties on, and I want to push those strappy little high heels around my shoulder and plunge into her deliciously hot center.

Serena pushes the skirt past her hips slowly, letting me savor the moment. The material caresses her curves as she bares herself to me. She lets the silk slide down her legs and pool at the floor along with the rest of her clothing. Completely bared to me. A vision that I will never tire of cherishing or ravishing.

I move my finger across the small remote used to control the vibrator I have buried in her backside, and the vibration deep inside of her begins to increase. I watch her shiver with anticipation as I discard my clothes and then guide her to our bed. "Lay back for me, tesoro, and show me what is mine. I want to see the diamond gleaming while it pleasures you," I say, laying her down and parting her legs so I can see the glistening of her center and the diamond end of the plug beneath it. I turn the vibration to a heavier pulse, and her eyes roll upward, hazy with desire after only a couple hours of anticipation.

She moans softly, causing my cock to throb with need.

I make her wait, increasing the ultimate pleasure that she gets, although waiting to bury myself in her heat and drive forward until she is screaming my name is also punishment for me. I slide my finger down her slit, dip into the cream-filled center, sliding in and out and teasing her unmercifully.

She moans, a soft little purr that makes my cock harden further, but I continue to tease. Only when she is moaning my name over and over and her hands have tightened against the bedding do I run the head of my cock up and down her slit, gathering the wetness on my length before nudging her opening. Her hips lift, but I tsk, shaking my head, holding her tight little belly down, and smacking her pussy so that she knows she doesn't take her own pleasure.

Her eyes spark with heated desire, and I bring my hand down several more times before slowly working myself in, teasing her with my length, but then thrusting deep because I want her to feel me at the very end of her, to feel me against the vibrator in her ass, and to know that I am the only one who will ever give her this kind of pleasure.

I lift her heels and place them over my shoulders, needing to bury myself deeper. She cries out with pleasure, and my dick throbs with need. Mine! That's all I can think about when I feel the end of her, and I hit it again and again until she is trembling on the end of my cock, soaking me with her desire.

I slide in and out slowly, adjusting the remote so that she feels the intensity of its probe, because I'm not nearly finished with her yet. Her ankles tighten against my neck, and with the next thrust I push my cock in deep, long and hard, sliding through her creaminess. I do it again and again, listening to her little sounds and watching as her eyes roll with desire. I drive deeper, harder, and faster, watching my beauty build again until she pants my name, thrashing that beautiful mane of dark hair all around her. Then she's trembling, shaking on the very end of my dick as I push in deeper, bending her in half to capture her mouth with my own. I swallow the scream of my name as she goes crashing over the edge, shaking and trembling while bringing me to a mind-numbing release as I fill her with my seed.

I lean my head against her forehead, rocking us both as we catch our breath and come down from the high we create when we are together. Never has it been this way for me, ever. This overwhelming feeling of absolute need to be Serena's everything.

My wife, I can barely believe it, and while it brings me great pride, it also gives me great pause about her security. I try to shake it off, kissing her beautifully swollen lips, and her eyes have closed. She is completely undone and exhausted from the day's events and our lovemaking. I head into the bathroom to clean up, and then clean her gently before pulling the covers over her body. I stroke her cheek as she sighs against my hand, letting me know she's fallen sound asleep. I slide on my clothes as quietly as I can, and then head into the main cabin, pouring myself a glass of wine before texting Antonio that I'm ready to talk to him and the security team.

He and Nate come out just a few moments later. "A drink?" I ask.

"Coke for me," Nate says as Antonio walks to the bar and grabs a water. He opens the refrigerator and hands a bottle of soda to Nate.

Antonio knows me well. "You need something, boss?" he asks, taking a long pull of his water.

"Yeah. How far behind are Salvatore and my great-uncle?"

Nate touches his phone and scrolls around a bit before replying. "They're about an hour behind us. They had a slight delay at the airport with takeoff, but we do have an update. The Europeans will be touching down about two hours after you and an hour after your great-uncle and Salvatore. We have a window of time before they land to get you and Serena to the resort and clamp down all internal security."

"What about the riders?" I ask, and I don't like the look on Nate's face one fucking bit, but he seems to recover his composure after a few moments. "We don't get paid to tell you lies or sugarcoat the truth. If Jay were here, he'd give it to you straight, and that's exactly what I'm going to do. We have a mess of gang runners screaming across the desert on their way to Vegas. Over four hundred riders who believe they're coming into the city to drop a load of product and pick up a package that Dominic needs delivered to his crew on Monday night in Vegas. We know for certain that they haven't been told what the package is, and you can be pretty certain that it's code for Serena," Nate says, and Antonio squashes the empty bottle of water in his hands and then throws it across the cabin.

While internally my rage is full-blown, I also know that the security team we've hired is the best in the world, and they have intel that until recently we did not have access to. "What's the plan?" I ask, calmer than I feel.

Nate nods. "We're working to understand exactly how Vicenti's drugs came into the country." I look at him incredulously because I couldn't give a fuck less about the South American cartel's drugs.

He raises a hand as if sensing my angst. "I know what you're thinking, and Serena is our top priority, but once we know how the product is getting imported, we'll be able to figure out how the dope got cut and who's responsible. We need to prove it was Alfreita Jr. if we want Vicenti's help. We could take Dominic out, just like you or your family could have, but that won't stop Alfreita Jr. He's going to keep coming, and he could have a hundred Dominic's with many more motorcycle crews. We need to get to the source and understand how the drugs come into the country and what happens to Vicenti's product. He's an honorable man. He may be dealing in a ton of heavy shit, but it's pure, not like the poison they're pushing, and when Vicenti finds out who is responsible, he will make it right."

I nod, taking it all in. This security team has proven themselves time and time again, but I can't sit around and wait until all the pieces of this miraculous plan come together. "Thanks, Nate. Carry on with the plan," I say, and he turns and walks into the security room with Antonio.

I send a message to Salvatore, knowing we're already in position.

> Ready the family in Vegas. All hell is about to break loose.

Chapter 30

Serena

I wake from a deep, sated sleep and glance around at our surroundings and out the windows of the Gulfstream. The sky is lit up in a magnificent show of pinks, purples, magentas, and oranges as the sun begins to descend. I glance at my phone and see that I've managed to sleep the entire flight away. I scowl at the spot next to me which barely looks touched, leaving me to wonder what Giovanni has been up to. I head into the shower and then go in search of him in the main cabin.

Giovanni's sitting at the small table by the oblong window, working on his laptop with a cup of coffee in front of him when I emerge from the bedroom. He glances up and smiles. "Good morning. How did you sleep, tesoro?" he asks, holding his hand out for me.

I cross the short distance, taking it as he turns in his chair, settles me into his lap, and kisses me lightly on the lips.

"I can't believe I slept the entire flight away. I must have been exhausted."

"Hmm. Making babies, it is hard work, no?" Giovanni says, running his finger down the length of my neck and settling onto my collarbone, stroking the tender flesh as he continues to gaze at me.

"I guess so," I say, just as the captain lets us know we are about forty minutes from landing.

I open my mouth in surprise. "I was just joking! I knew what time it was, but I didn't really think I slept the entire flight away!"

Giovanni laughs, pushing my hair back from my face. "You needed the sleep, and now you need to eat before we land," he says, texting something on his phone.

In a matter of moments, one of the service attendants pushes a silver cart laden with silver domed dishes into the main cabin. I don't know her, but she's wearing the same uniform that just months ago I was wearing, providing the same service that I provided for the most influential people in the world until I met Giovanni.

She places our food on the table, removes the lids, and then pours our coffee. "Orzo for you, I'm told," she says.

I crinkle my nose at the decaffeinated beverage, but it smells nutty and oh so wonderful, so I nod to the nice attendant. "Baby on board," I say by way of explanation, and she smiles widely.

"Congratulations! Would you like anything else?" she asks kindly.

I shake my head, laughing as I take in all that Giovanni has ordered. "I think this little breakfast for dinner feast will be enough," I say, glancing up to find him watching me with a broad smile.

We usually have a latte and quick sweet for breakfast, but this meal is nothing like that. He picks up one of the plates filled with baked eggs and prosciutto and places a generous serving on my plate, then adds a cream-filled pastry and a large helping of assorted mixed fruit.

"You seriously expect me to eat all of this?"

"You need nourishment, and so does our child," Giovanni says, forking a bite of the egg dish and lifting it to my lips.

I take a bite and almost moan with contentment. If only we didn't have someone trying to hunt me down and ruin Giovanni, our lives would be perfect. I never eat this much at one time, but I am ravenous and manage to consume every morsel that he puts on my plate and lifts to my lips.

When the captain announces our landing in approximately ten

minutes, the service attendants come into the room and clear our plates, hauling everything out of the cabin. Giovanni takes my hand and guides me to the reclining seats by another set of windows before buckling me in.

I yawn, and his forehead crinkles with concern. "I have no idea how I can be tired again after just sleeping for so long. Maybe it's all the food you gave me," I say.

He nods. "Rest and nourishment are probably good for you both. There will be plenty of time for rest when we reach the resort," he says as the plane begins its final descent, and the vast desert below comes into view.

In just a short time, the wheels hit the runway, and we are careening down the concrete path, watching the reddish landscape pass us by until the pilot dramatically slows his course of speed, and we taxi onto the private tarmac.

The security guards come out of their room and open the landing door for us and then quickly surround us as we make our way to the awaiting helicopter, which proudly displays The Larussio emblem.

Once on board, the pilot lifts up and we are soon making our way down over the city. I watch as some of the peripheral casinos come into view and recognize some of the more famous names, and then I see it, The Larussio, and from the air the sprawling resort and casino dwarfs the entire block with its footprint, with towers reaching high into the sky.

I am so excited that I point, and Giovanni smiles broadly. "It's definitely a vision," he says proudly.

The flight is brief from the airport, and the pilot lands with expert precision on one of the flat towers of The Larussio. The security guards jump out with Giovanni right behind them, and he turns to grab my waist and hoist me out of the helicopter before we are guided to the rooftop door and down a private elevator to our penthouse suite.

Giovanni makes his way to the granite kitchen bar and greets all of the security men who are sitting around the dining room table. They're all focused on the double-sided monitor that's slowly lowering into the middle of the table from an open ceiling panel above. He pours himself an espresso, and grabs a bottle of water and a banana from the massive fruit bowl on the counter and hands them to me.

"Water instead of espresso? Giovanni, this is so not fair. Maybe caffeine deprivation is making me so tired," I say, pretending to pout.

He leans down and kisses my lips and whispers in my ear, "I ordered decaf from room service and a light snack for everyone. It should arrive shortly. Relax a bit and let me deal with what needs to be done, tesoro," he says as his phone begins to vibrate.

I sit with him at the kitchen bar until room service arrives with my drink, and cheese, sausage, and fruit trays for the entire group. When he finally gets off the phone, he starts to talk with the men.

Antonio glances at me and then back to Giovanni. "Are you sure you want Serena to be part of this?"

Giovanni's eyes narrow at Antonio, but then turn to me and soften. "I would prefer you sheltered from what transpires shortly, but if you need to be a part of it, I will not deny you."

He glances down as his phone vibrates with a message. "Salvatore and Great-Uncle are on their way up."

They walk in together moments later with an entourage of security. Do I really want to know what the father of my child is about to do in order to keep us safe? Will it change the way I feel about him? Katarina has told me how her mother overheard her father putting a hit out on someone, not realizing that if he didn't, the men would have killed her mom. I have seen the protection and love that Giovanni and his family bring to me and my family, even after years of believing they were the enemy, and like Katarina, I realize how fortunate we are to have men in our lives who will do whatever it takes to protect the women they love.

"I'm going to rest for a short while, and then Kate, Jenny, Marenah, and Sasha are coming over. They should be landing a little later in the evening. They plan to get a bite to eat and get settled in their rooms. Kate and Chase are already here, and the ladies will pick Kate up on the way over. And, Giovanni, there's no need for me to hear this conversation. I trust you with all of my heart."

His eyes fill with emotion. "Gentlemen, start the meeting. I'll be with you shortly," he says, scooping me from the stool and into his arms, then carrying me into the bedroom.

Giovanni kicks the door closed and lays me on the bed before sliding in next to me and pulling me close. "Tell me you meant that; tell me that you trust me and my family to keep you and our child safe," he says, kissing my forehead and pushing my hair off my face.

"I meant it, Giovanni. I'm sorry it took me this long. Perhaps I just needed to understand how Katarina's mom, Karissa, felt when she left the family. She loved her husband when she married him, but she didn't know that he was part of the family. She heard him put a hit out and fled. Katarina spent her life without her father, and Karissa spent her life pining away for her love. That is not what I want for us. I've told you—ensure that our family is safe. I promise, come tomorrow, I will still be by your side."

Chapter 31

Gio

I will safeguard Serena and our child with everything and everyone at my disposal, but if for some reason things don't go as planned, she needs to be prepared. Salvatore has spent weeks teaching her self-defense moves, and she may choose to use them, regardless of how much I may wish it weren't so.

"Tesoro, you will rest. I will take care of what needs to be done. I know that you have trained with Salvatore, but if there comes a time that you are taken, what do you do, now that you are with child?" I ask.

She looks at me like that option hasn't even crossed her mind. "I can't risk a fight being pregnant, can I?"

I pull her close and kiss her lips. "No, tesoro, I'm sure there are methods, but you have not been trained in those. If it ever comes to them taking you, then you do not fight like Salvatore taught you. You wait. You do not give them any reason to anger. You wait until we rescue you; understand?"

She nods, but the frightened look on her face is not the one I want to see. "Giovanni, until just this moment, if they would have come for me, I would have given my life quickly so they couldn't hurt you, but now, our baby, I would have to fight until the end."

"You will not fight. You will not, Serena; do you understand? I will be the one who will fight and ensure you and our family's security," Giovanni says.

Serena nods, and I pull her close. She reaches up to kiss me on the lips. "Giovanni, do you think you will find them, get rid of them, and we'll be able to be a family?"

"Ssh. Tesoro, we will find them, and when we do, they will never threaten you and our child again, understand?" I say, but it kills me inside to think of the fear she must be in, not only for herself but now for the life she carries. I breathe deeply, drawing the strength I will need from the fear that is so visible on her face.

Serena nods. "I understand. Do not worry, Giovanni," she says, looking up at me with those expressive brown eyes that are full of love and trust.

I remain where I am, stroking her cheek for just a few more moments, soaking in her beauty and her fear and her strength, drawing upon it for what must be done.

When I return to the dining room, Salvatore and Great-Uncle look grim.

"Something is wrong; tell me," I demand, glancing from one to the other of them, but for what seems like hours to me neither of th*em* says a goddamn word.

Great-Uncle is the first to speak. "The security teams have picked up another gang coming in from the mountains. All in total 700 bikers, Giovanni."

My jaw tightens, but I know we are ready. "We have all our crews in place?" I ask Salvatore.

He nods. "And then some. Uncle Carlos called in his crews too. Mancini is sending a message not only to us but to Uncle Carlos to get out of his town. He thinks of Vegas as his, but Uncle Carlos has far-reaching arms and had his teams drive in from New York, Jersey, and Chicago and the entire Midwest. We are prepared in all respects, Giovanni."

Salvatore's phone buzzes. "See for yourself," he says, smiling widely as he gestures for us to join him at the window.

Great-Uncle and I walk over and look down at the Strip below, and for as far as the eye can see is a parade of motorcycles.

"Ours?" I ask, unable to see colors from this distance.

"Indeed. They're sending a message. If Dominic's crews head into this city, they're going to hit a rumbling wall of resistance," Salvatore says.

The light changes, and the brigade moves forward, slowly making their way into the city. We watch for more than ten minutes, and the parade hasn't ended yet. The reign of the Larussios is staggering. I gaze out over the vast city filled with a wall of riders. If I didn't fully understand its magnitude before, I certainly do now.

My phone buzzes, and I take the call from Jay. "The crews just hit town; in case you didn't feel the ground rumbling beneath you."

"We're watching now, Jay. Let me include Sal and Great-Uncle in the call."

"Sounds good."

"We have everyone on the line now," I say, a second after engaging the speaker.

"Good evening. Quick update for everyone. We've detained the Europeans at the airport. The team needs the family's direction on what you want done with them," Jay says.

Great-Uncle gestures to the two of us that he'll handle the conversation. Salvatore raises his eyebrows in question at me, but I don't know what he's about to say either. "I was in touch with Vicenti. He is grateful for the knowledge we were able to provide, feels responsible, and believes this is his wrong to right. They will be held, no harm. He and his team will be here in the next few hours. They will deal with the Europeans and Alfreita over the product situation. In turn, we will deal with the riders Dominic has sent, first and foremost to ensure Serena's safety, and second to ensure that poison those men are trafficking does not reach our city for distribution," Great-Uncle says, and I do not miss the underlying message. If it wasn't before, Vegas is the Larussios' city now.

"You've spoken with Uncle Carlos?" Salvatore asks.

"He and I have conferred, and he placed the order. This is his city now, and he wants to keep it safe. His soldiers have strict orders. Jay, we have a ton of manpower out there, willing and able to do your bidding. Security for Serena is priority; you tell us what we need to know or to have done," Great-Uncle says, and it's my turn to raise my eyebrows. Great-Uncle giving over control to the security team, he must really feel very confident in their abilities and allegiance to the family.

Jay starts to speak, but Great-Uncle isn't finished, and both Sal and I smile widely. He may have given the indication of giving up control, but he is far from ready for that. "We need to set up a meet, neutral territory, security ensured for travel to and from. You both need to attend, and Serena will stay here with Antonio and Nate," Great-Uncle says, and although I know that this is the safest place for her to be, the thought of her without me if something happens sends a panic straight to my chest.

Salvatore must see the alarm in my eyes and touches my shoulder. "We'll have a whole army of security men surrounding The Larussio, and guards with her and the ladies tonight. They won't get within two blocks of this resort," he says, and Great-Uncle nods.

"Salvatore is right. If one of you could remain behind, we would allow it, but you must meet as a formidable front to those who oppose us. Vicenti knows that he will be dealing with the two of you when I pass, and this may not be over for some time. It is time, especially for something as important as this, that I step back and allow you to take the reins. You must both attend the meeting," Great-Uncle says. I know the protocols, the rules that our families have lived by for so many generations, and this one, especially when it means relationships with our Colombian friends, is critical and cannot be ignored.

We finish making the arrangements that weren't finalized on the flight, and Great-Uncle finally leaves us to rest in his penthouse. I am more than impressed with our cousins' ability to organize and get their teams deployed throughout the city.

We have just pulled our enforcers and bosses into a conference call when Serena comes out of the bedroom. Jay and the security team are sitting around the large dining room table, and maps of the city are spread out everywhere. She glances around at the monitors above the table and takes in the pauses in conversation while everyone waits to see if they should continue.

"Sorry, I'm just going to grab a couple bottles of water. I'll take them into the bedroom and read or something until the ladies arrive," Serena says, making her way to the refrigerator.

She downs almost half a bottle of water in a few swallows. I know the feeling. It's so fucking dry in this desert. "Give us a few minutes and then continue, gentlemen," I say, leaving the table and joining her at the refrigerator.

I take a bunch of grapes and cheese from the tray and place them on a small plate, then hand her another bottle of water just as she finishes her first. "Take this with you. I'll bring you a snack," I say, and she gets the message, raises up on tiptoes, and kisses my lips lightly before taking her water back to the bedroom, seemingly fine with the fact that I don't want her to hear any part of the shit we're talking about right now.

I watch her until she is no longer in sight, and I glance over, feeling Sal's eyes on me. Something passes across his features that's impossible to understand. He looks away first, pulled back into the conversation with our men as I finish making her plate, adding a few chunks of cheese and crackers, and then go to find her in the bedroom.

She's settled into the big armchair in the corner, curled up with a blanket covering her, and has already started on the second bottle of water. "Is the air conditioning too cold for you, tesoro?" I ask, placing the snack on the table beside her.

"It's a little cool, but it's fine, Giovanni, and the blanket is perfect," Serena says, smiling at me. The temperature in the desert is so hot that the air conditioning is necessary, unlike in Italy.

"I'll have the temperature turned up a bit. I don't want you getting sick. I need to go out for a while, but it shouldn't be too long. The security team will remain with you and the girls once they arrive. Text me if you need anything until then," I tell her, kissing her lips one more time.

When I break our kiss, she looks up at me and grasps the sides of my face with her hands. "Giovanni Larussio, I love you so much. Go, do what you must. I will be here when you return," she says, kissing my lips lightly.

My heart constricts tighter than it has before as I leave her in the hands of security, walk into the dining room, and tell the men, "Let's go."

Chapter 32

─────────

Serena

My cell phone dings, and I glance down at it and smile broadly. My friends have all arrived in Vegas and are on their way up. They have serious protection and are on strict orders not to be anywhere outside of the resort or away from their bodyguards, but they can come and visit me as long as security stays with us. I almost fly into the bathroom, not realizing how excited I am to see them and all the pictures they captured of the wedding that we want to show Kate.

I freshen up quickly, slide into my sandals, and head out into the dining room, where Antonio and Nate have taken up residence at the table.

"Hey, Sasha, Jenny, Kate, and Marenah are coming up. Do you mind if we take over the table so we can visit?" I ask, heading to the refrigerator to take out a few bottles of wine coolers and some lemonade that was delivered earlier, placing them in a large bowl that I fill with ice, and then open a bottle of red to breathe before they arrive. I head into the living room to the fully stocked bar and bring back a bottle of vodka. Marenah isn't much into wine, but she likes vodka in just about anything.

The doorbell rings, and I rush across the dining room, into the

185

living room to make my way to the door, but I'm not fast enough for Antonio or Nate.

"Whoa," Nate says. I know you're excited, but if we go against protocol here, your husband's liable to have us fed to the sharks," he says, his eyes dancing.

"There aren't any sharks here in the desert, more likely the coyotes," I say, earning me a wide grin from Antonio. "Are you going to answer the door?" I ask, gesturing to where that big double set of doors stands between me and my friends who I have so much to catch up with.

"Far be it for me to stand in between a lady and her gab session," Nate says, checking his phone before opening the door to my friends, who literally push past him to get to me. Sasha is the first through the door, and she hugs me tight, followed by Marenah, Kate, and Jenny.

They come in followed by an entourage of security who veer off to join Antonio and Nate in the living room as I lead my friends into the dining room. "I can't believe you all came," I say, spinning around to see them.

"Those men couldn't keep us away no matter what their security issues," Kate says, and Sasha has the good grace to look embarrassed because her boyfriend, Jay, is the head of security and running point on this assignment, and we all know that he is a stickler for protocols, probably as bad as Great-Uncle and Salvatore.

"How did you ever manage to get Chase to let you out for the evening?" I ask Kate as she slowly lowers herself and her large swollen belly into the dining room chair.

"Oh, I have my ways," she says coyly, batting her eyelashes at us.

We all laugh at our auburn-haired friend with bright blue eyes who is so pregnant that she can barely bend. "Here, use this for your feet," Jenny says, scooting another chair around so Kate can use it for a footstool.

"If you want, we can go into the living room and have the guys work in here," I say, not having thought that Kate may not be as comfortable at the table, but she smiles at me widely and shakes her head.

"No, it's fine, really. I have done absolutely nothing but keep my feet up since the early labor incident, and we're doing fine. The doctor says I'm well past the stage of concern for multiples, so anytime they want to make their presence known, they won't be in danger, and we couldn't be in a better place for it to happen. The doctor on staff here knows my OB-GYN, and I think Chase and my parents actually like the idea of us staying here until the babies are born. I have to admit, it's been nice to be on site and look out at the developments of the resort around me as the days go by," Kate says.

The ladies dig in to the snacks, sandwiches, and beverages that I've laid out, and then want to watch the wedding video they created from the pictures that were taken. "Hang on; I don't know how to use this monitor," I say, gesturing to the ceiling. They look up at the tiled white ceiling and back to me.

I walk into the living room to find the guys laughing over a shared joke. "Hey, can one of you help us lower the monitor in the dining room so we can watch the wedding video?" I ask.

Antonio stands and gestures for the rest of them to stay seated. "I've got this, boys. Carry on with your fun," he says, still smiling as he walks with me into the dining room and takes in all the drinks and laughter of my friends.

Antonio pushes a button on the remote control, the ceiling panels open, and the monitor is lowered over the table so both sides can see the screen. "Whoa, seriously high tech," Jenny says.

"Giovanni sent me the link to the video to put in the archives. You want me to pull it up for you?" Antonio asks me.

"Yes, please. I have it on my phone, but I have no clue how to get it from there to that," I say, gesturing to the overhead.

He smiles and runs through a few menu bars, and soon the wedding is about to begin. "There you go, ladies; enjoy," Antonio says, sauntering into the living room to leave us to our drinks and wedding fun.

I watch the video, still absolutely mesmerized by the look of passion in Giovanni's eyes that the camera has managed to capture as I walk down the stairs, through the great room, and into the wide-open double doors of the chapel on my brother's arm. When the wedding video is over, all my newfound friends are drying their eyes.

"If you guys keep this up, you are going to make me cry. You know it doesn't take much these days, pregnancy and all," I say, and clap my hands over my ears as their squeals of excitement pierce the air.

"Stop already!" I laugh.

"Why didn't you tell us? When did you find out? Why are the besties always the last to know?"

I am laughing so hard that tears roll down my face. "We seriously just figured it out. In fact, we haven't even had blood work taken to confirm it yet. We left so quickly after the wedding. I believe Giovanni plans on having the physician that you see here run the lab work," I say, addressing Kate.

"You will absolutely love her. She's been a gem the entire time we've been here, and she was the one who was able to stop the labor in the first place. I thank God for her every day. In fact, she was just contracted to stay on the grounds as The Larussio physician until the final grand opening, but Chase is trying to convince her to stay on even longer than that," Kate says.

"Maybe Giovanni can help too! And speaking of grand opening, we should probably help you and Jenny get ready for that event. What do you guys need help with between now and Friday night?" I ask, pouring myself another glass of water.

Sasha, who is a ballerina and seldom drinks anything but water or tea, holds out her glass for more but then lowers it slowly as her eyes begin to roll, and her mouth opens to say something, but nothing comes out.

It's like things are happening in slow motion, and with a sense of dread I realize that something is terribly, terribly wrong because none of my friends are talking, and each and every one of them looks like I feel. A floating sensation overtakes me at the same time I realize that Mancini has won, and I may never see my husband again or unborn child come into this world.

Chapter 33

Gio

Salvatore and I are escorted down the security elevator and into the lower-level parking ramp, one floor lower than the guest parking area and reserved for our family. When we are secured in the awaiting limo, Matt, Dereck, and Nick are all with us. Two in the front and one in the rear seats with Sal and me sitting on the middle bench seat of the impressive stretch, and our cousins and security team have surrounded us as we make our way out onto the Strip.

"We've just received confirmation that all teams are in place. Our crew members and allies have taken over every establishment on the Strip, and Capone, their president, and his leaders are already at the warehouse where we'll meet. The Desert Riders are about two hours out, but Ryker, their president, and his leaders are on their way to meet with us, and the Europeans are on ice, awaiting Vicenti's orders," Jay says.

"Very good. The rest of the cousins from Italy are just landing. They'll meet us there in case backup is needed," Sal says.

Dereck is driving and makes his way to the other side of the Strip, exiting on a ramp that leads out to nothing but desert. The limo eventually pulls off the highway and onto a gravel road that leads to a large old metal warehouse. Dereck navigates us close to the door on the side of the building. We are not the first to arrive, as there are twelve large motorcycles parked outside. "You good with the number of men?" I ask to no one in particular.

Matt turns in his seat and looks at me. "Those bikes belong to the president and leaders of your club and the Desert Riders. These are the men who are going to make things happen today, and we have a plan to make sure they do. You're in good hands, Mr. Larussio."

"Thanks, and the name is Gio," I tell him, taking in our isolated environment as they jump out of the car, opening the doors before surrounding me and Sal as we approach the building and walk in. Sal and the cousins usually deal with things such as this alone, but we are talking about Serena's life. If things go wrong, they will answer to me, and if things don't go according to plan, Vicenti's going to want to deal with the members of the family he is familiar with and the one who will take the Don's place.

Salvatore is confident and comfortable with the lifestyle and is the first to walk up to the president of the Larussio club, The Rivalry, extending his hand in greeting before introducing us, one by one, to Capone. He is a tall intense-looking bald-headed man with piercing gray eyes and has a bandana tied around his forehead and nods tersely to each of us as we are introduced. He is wearing black leather pants and boots and is bare chested other than a leather cut. His muscled body is covered with tattoos that trail down his neck and cover both arms, and he is flanked by five of his club brothers who are all dressed similarly and stand tense across from their rivals.

Sal then turns, extends his hand in greeting, and introduces the two of us to the tall fully tatted man wearing a black leather vest and pants.

"I'm Ryker, president of the Desert Riders," the man says, extending his hand to us, one at a time, while his own club brothers stand at the ready beside him.

"Gentlemen, I appreciate you meeting with us on such short notice. I won't waste your time and will get right to the point." Sal turns his attention to Ryker. "We understand your crew is staunchly opposed to running anything but pure product in your cities. Unfortunately, we've become aware that your crew is now running tainted product for Mancini," Sal says.

Ryker runs his hands over the five o'clock scruff he's wearing, and his bright blue eyes narrow. "We only run with the pure stuff and do our best to keep the streets safe," he says, his men all seemingly tense and ready to move at a movement's notice.

"Until now," Sal says.

"Are you telling me we picked up bad product?"

"That's what we understand, why we wanted to talk to you ourselves. We believe your intentions are good, but the product you're carrying is cut with poison. We won't allow it on our streets," Sal says.

Ryker's jaw tightens, and the bright blue eyes narrow at the two of us suspiciously. "My crew doesn't run anything that's not pure. We take this accusation very seriously, and clearly you do or you obviously wouldn't be here to relay the message yourself."

Sal nods. "Innocent people will die if the product you and your men are carrying hits our streets," Sal says, and I don't think Capone misses the possessive term of *our streets*.

Ryker nods, contemplating before he speaks. "If the product my men are packing is cut, the delivery will not proceed. I'm going to need proof; we can test it together, and I'm open to having one of your test kits used. If we were given tainted shit, Dominic Mancini won't live to see another day," he says.

If that product tests positive for the poison that it's rumored to be cut with, we all know we have much larger problems than Mancini, but the president can deal with him when we're ready, and Vicenti can help us deal with Alfreita.

"Fair enough; let's get this shit tested," Sal says, and one of Capone's men breaks formation to retrieve a plastic-wrapped brick of white product and a testing kit, which he lays on the table.

"Break the seal," Ryker says to one of his leaders who's already wielding his pocketknife, ready to cut into the thin overlay. He pricks the edge and slides his blade along the seam, inserts the tip into the drug, and brings out a thin film of the white product with his knife.

His partner holds out the clear glass vial from the kit filled a third of the way with a pink-colored solution. Ryker tells him to add the product, and Capone nods in agreement. The minute the product hits the solution, it turns blue, and one of the men standing in the rear raises his eyebrows. "Seems like pure cocaine to me," he says.

Ryker turns and glares at his insolent and ill-informed leader. "That used to be enough, but we're not done. Watch and learn," Ryker says as the man who just put the cocaine in the vial adds another liquid that turns the solution back to pink. "Cobalt thiocyanate will tell us if there's cocaine, the blue reaction was positive. Hydrochloric acid will neutralize it and allow us to see how much is pure, and how much is not," he says as the man breaks another vial and adds it. The solution immediately breaks into two layers, one blue layer at the bottom and another pink, larger layer at the top.

Ryker's eyes narrow and darken as he watches the solution. "I'll contact my crews and have them stop all anticipated distribution."

"Excellent. We have our reasons, but we don't want Mancini taken out until we give the word, and as for the product, I have it on good authority that you will be compensated for your losses," Sal says.

"That's more than generous, Mr. Larussio," Ryker says, reaching out to shake hands with Sal.

"Our intel has your cell; we'll contact you when we know more. In the meantime, I'd like to avoid an all-out gang war in our city," Sal says.

"Our men are in place all over the city; no doubt you saw them when you and your leaders arrived. They knew you and a few of your men were coming to meet with us, but if any more come riding into town, they're not going to stop and ask questions," Sal says, leaving out the fact that we also know about the order to take Serena to Dominic's men.

Ryker nods, and his face turns grim. "I understand how this looks, but I would never have my crews peddling that poison," he says, gesturing to the vial still on the wooden table in front of us.

Sal's eyes grow dark and intense, because it's Ryker's job to know exactly what he's pushing, which he didn't, but Sal doesn't antagonize the man; he lets him think about what he just said.

It doesn't take him long to catch up. "When we accept the shipment, it's tested at the time, and then again when we accept it on this side of the ocean, granted randomly, but enough that this couldn't have just slipped by. Only my top men are entrusted with this job, and they pay certain people, which means I have a much bigger problem on my hands. I'll look into it, and the Desert Riders will be instructed to turn back, unless of course you want some extra help. My understanding is that Dominic wants your woman," Ryker says, gesturing to me.

My jaw tightens, and I'm not near as diplomatic as Sal has been through the course of the negotiations. "You accepted a job to kidnap my wife?" I ask, because if he and his crew signed on to take Serena to Dominic's men, he will be a dead man before he's had time to walk out of this goddamn building.

"No sir, Mr. Larussio. Our job was to move product, but we understand a rival gang from California is riding in to make trouble on the Strip and capture your wife. We were heading into town ready to deliver product, no doubt about that, but we didn't learn about Dominic's plan until just shortly ago. Like I said, if your teams need help, I'll offer my crew's assistance," Ryker says.

Capone doesn't look pleased with the idea of playing nice with the Desert Riders, and he glares at Ryker with pure disdain, but he knows where his orders are coming from and remains quiet as Sal and I silently consider the options.

Sal looks to me to see if I want to take lead, but I shake my head, urging him to continue. He has a good head on his shoulders for this work, just like our great-uncle, and in more ways than one I wish he had been the older of the cousins and were next in line for Don of the family.

Sal starts to speak just as I glance down at an incoming text from Jay. I cut Sal off with trembling hands and a tightened chest. "Serena and Sasha have both been taken. We're going to need your help, gentlemen," I say to both of the motorcycle gang presidents and their leaders.

Chapter 34

Jay

A text comes through from Nate just as an alert comes through my phone that the HVAC system has been compromised in the penthouse tower, where he and the others are guarding the ladies.

gassed

Son of a bitch! I alert our intel to turn on the cameras in the penthouse and get our other teams into the systems double time. In less than three minutes I have eyes on the entire penthouse, and I and all of our team grab our protective gear and double time it across the resort to storm the room.

The ladies are seated around the table, and their heads are lying on the table. I don't know if they're dead or alive, and I only count three: Kate, Jenny and Marenah. My chest tightens at the realization that both Serena and Sasha are missing.

I instruct intel to make a sweep of the entire condo while I check the pulse on Kate, Jenny and Marenah, call for an ambulance, and help our team carry the ladies out of the gas-filled condo while we wait for reinforcements to arrive.

Antonio and Nate are both passed out on the floor, one gripping a cell and one with his cell out and right in front of him on the floor, along with the others. The men drag them out to the hall.

I still don't see the other women, the one my team and I have been hired to protect, and the one who means the world to me.

I instruct intel to do a walk-through of every single hall and escape-way while I send a message to Gio and Chase, letting them know that Serena and Sasha were taken and that the other ladies were left unconscious but not hurt. Then I connect with Giovanni, who is in the middle of negotiations with the president of the Desert Riders.

"Where the fuck are they?" Giovanni roars, and I feel the same intense fear that I know he's going through knowing that some deranged psycho has our women, but we don't have the luxury of time or explanation if we're going to get them back.

We have no time; that will come later. "Put me on speakerphone and include the presidents," I growl, and Giovanni does as I ask without hesitation. "I need all exits and entrance points to the city blocked. No one gets in or out right now; shut this fucking city down," I roar, knowing goddamn well that Sal and his cousins will have already sent out instruction to the teams they have on standby throughout the city.

Ryker is the first to speak, and I don't need a confirmation from Capone, who I know is already passing the instruction to his crews as we speak. "I'm sending the order out now," Ryker says.

"Roger that! Next, the airport and every helipad in this town. I need a mass infiltration, a huge diversion. Set those goddamn runways on fire if you have to, but no one gets in the air!"

"Ryker and I will cover that together," Capone says, letting me know that he and his men are willing to work side by side with the Desert Riders.

"Next—Sal, I have no quick jurisdiction in the prison systems. If you do, I wouldn't wait for Vicenti to take Mancini out. I'd get to the fucker right the hell now and use every means necessary to find out where our women are."

"I've got that shit covered. He'll be taken in less than five minutes, and you can bet your ass he'll fucking talk," Ryker says.

"Roger that; just keep him alive! Everyone stay at the warehouse, give directions from there, and keep the family safeguarded," I say to the motorcycle leaders and my team. "I need to disconnect and handle intel. We will get the ladies back," I say, disconnecting before Gio or his wild-ass cousin have a chance to intervene.

In less than three minutes, the bikes can all be heard howling through the city. All exits, main thoroughfares, and even side streets are filled with riders. I get the message that all the helicopter pads are covered, a gang war has erupted at the airport, the runways are on fire, and all flights have been grounded. They'll think we think they're trying to head out of town, but I know better.

The motherfucker we caught on camera and just ran facial recognition on is none other than one of Gio and Salvatore's oldest cousin's best friends. The only way the cousin stayed off our radar was to have someone else do his dirty work, but it's over now. The trackers the ladies wear allow me and my men to follow them right through the HVAC system and toward the other end of the resort.

As soon as our men get the tracer on, we have the entire tower surrounded, and before they even come out of the system that winds its way through the complex, we have the door surrounded. Two men walk out holding Serena and Sasha's listless forms in their arms, meaning to head directly into the condo to the right. The very same unit that was reserved with a credit card that led right back to Giovanni and Salvatore's cousin's best friend, one of the fuckers standing in front of me holding my angel in his arms.

The Larussios have just lost the right to kill these fuckers themselves, and with two quick shots to their heads, they fall to the floor. Cole catches Serena before she falls, knowing she's with child, while I catch Sasha. The other men are surrounding us, and I order a sweep of the entire HVAC system.

"Tell me Serena's alive," I say to Cole, feeling Sasha's faint but rhythmic pulse under my thumb as I stroke her neck.

"She's alive, just sleeping like a baby," he says, and my heart finally seems to start beating again.

I slide down to the floor and hold Sasha in my arms, and Cole checks Serena for any other injuries while I get Giovanni on the line.

"We have the ladies. They're still out cold, but they're breathing and haven't been harmed. We're on the way to the urgent care facility on-site. If you want your doctor to examine Serena, we'll be there in less than ten minutes; otherwise I can call someone else in," I say.

"No, her doctor is on call this entire week because she's here. Take her down, and we'll meet you there, but the entire city is a nightmare. It will take us a while to get to the other side of the city in this mess," Giovanni says.

"I know boss, I know. Have Ryker bring you in, all the traffic ways are congested. He'll get you here the quickest," I say, and smile broadly because our ladies are safe, and the thought of Giovanni Larussio on the back of a motorcycle gang bike is something that I would pay a great deal of money to see.

Chapter 35

Gio

"Jay said your crew should get us to the resort," I say, looking at Ryker, and Capone looks shocked that our security team would want me to ride back with the Desert Rider president and not himself.

"You have something to say?" Sal asks him.

"No, we have every exit blocked, but the main streets are a nightmare, and the Riders actually know Vegas like the back of their hands. You're safe with them," Capone says.

Ryker's cell phone buzzes, and he glances down at an incoming message. "We've got Dominic and he's starting to talk. Let's get you to the resort and reunited with your woman, and we can talk about what comes next once we're there," Ryker says, walking toward the back and returning with two helmets. He throws one to both Sal and me. "One rides with me; one rides with Capone. We go in united," Ryker says, and our president looks at him with newfound respect and nods his agreement.

Sal looks to me with a big grin. He's enjoying this shit just a little too much. I narrow my eyes at him as we're escorted out the door and both hop onto the back of the huge Harleys, and they roar to life. The presidents and road captains of both crews lead the way, and both presidents follow them with us on the back. There is a wall of stalled traffic—cars, buses, and tourist vans, along with a sea of bikers—congesting the streets of downtown Las Vegas, but the men weave easily in between vehicles to continue our way forward.

Ryker's crew heads down back roads that lead to more back roads, avoiding the main thoroughfares, and pull up to the back of The Larussio emergency ambulance entrance that is right around the corner from the urgent center at the resort.

I get off the bike and shake hands with Ryker. "I owe you a debt of gratitude. Hang around the city; we have much to discuss," I say, before racing into the entrance with Sal on my heels and making our way down the long hall and into the medical facility.

There is a receptionist on duty, but I don't even stop, leaving Sal to deal with formalities as I burst through the doors that I know Serena's behind. Jay is on the other side of the room, hovering over Sasha, who is lying on one of the hospital beds.

Serena's physician, Dr. Palento, has already arrived and is taking her vitals while Cole stands next to her with his hand on her pulse. I nod to him, and he moves aside. I place my finger on her pulse with one hand and shake his with the other because speaking at this moment is not something that I can do.

Her physician glances up at me. "Your head of security alerted us to the fact that Mrs. Larussio is with child, in case we needed special services. She and the baby are fine," she says just as Salvatore bursts through the door and stalks over to us.

"How is she?" he asks gruffly, taking in Serena's pallor and body's stillness.

"She and the baby are fine," I say, taking in the slow expanse of his chest and the quiet exhale of his breath. As tough on the exterior as Salvatore is, family means everything to him.

"You can't just burst in here like that. You could cause either of the ladies to scare as they come into consciousness, and we need to keep Serena calm. She's with child," Dr. Palento says, turning from us and putting her stethoscope to Serena's chest as she finishes her exam. "Serena will be waking up shortly. Anyone who's not family should vacate the room so she's not overwhelmed when she wakens.

I don't want her blood pressure any higher than it is," she says, glancing pointedly at Sal.

Salvatore glares at her. "I'm family and the godfather to their child," he says, and I raise my eyebrows since we haven't even talked about that yet.

"I guess you can stay, but take care not to scare her," Dr. Palento says, bustling around the table and then heading to the other side of the room to talk to Jay about Sasha.

"Whoa, is she intense," Sal says, scowling, still taking in the physician as she marches across the room, intent on caring for both of her patients.

I hadn't really noticed, but before I can say a word, Serena's head moves from side to side, and she takes a large gulp of air. "Gio, they're here…"

Son of a bitch, the first thing she recalls is the horror of them overtaking her. The bastards will pay for the fear they've caused my dark-haired beauty. "I want that son of a bitch dead now," I growl, low enough that only Sal can hear my wrath.

He nods, and I know it will be done as he walks over to where Jay and Serena's physician are talking, leaving me alone with Serena as her eyes slowly open. Her entire body jerks as she comes awake, and I place my finger back on her pulse, already knowing it's beating faster than it should. I stroke her lips with my other finger. "Serena, it's me, Giovanni. It's over, tesoro. You and the baby are fine," I say, continuing to stroke her neck right over her pulse, hoping to calm her as she fully wakens and realizes what happened.

Her eyes open wider, and she takes me in, and then her eyes fill with tears as she remembers. "The baby, our baby is okay?"

"Shh, tesoro, our little one is perfectly fine. You, on the other hand, need to calm down. Your pulse is racing too fast, Serena."

She nods, coming to even more. "Dammit, we were just having girl time, in our own house. Is this why you make me wear a tracker?" she asks, and I wish it weren't so, but I can't deny it. All I can do is pull her to my chest as the tears begin to fall, and she sobs against me.

Her physician turns, noticing, says a few more words to Jay, and then walks toward us. "She's distraught, why?" she asks.

"Well, clearly because some lunatic has just kidnapped her," Sal says, joining our group.

She glares at him and tosses her long blonde ponytail before pushing up the sleeves of the white Henley she's wearing underneath the red Larussio scrubs. She adjusts the remote and raises Serena into a sitting position. She checks Serena's pulse and listens to her chest as Antonio and Nate burst in, both looking hazy and drugged, their eyes darting back and forth, taking in the bodies of Serena and Sasha.

Nate heads toward Jay and Sasha, and Antonio heads toward us. He shakes his head as he looks down at her tear-stricken face. "I am so goddamn sorry. We never realized the gas was filling the room until it was too late," Antonio says.

"It's not your fault; it doesn't even matter. Time and time again they will come for us, and time and time again the family will outsmart them. The Larussios will always win," Serena says, taking me completely by surprise as her petite blonde physician glares up at both me and Sal.

An hour later, the ladies are cleared to leave the urgent care center. They are both anxious to go home and check on their friends, who are safely with their men, and Serena's blood pressure has finally returned to normal. Sasha sits nuzzling into Jay's shoulder as he holds her close and continues to text out orders to handle loose ends. The ladies are both placed in wheelchairs, and Jay and I push them out of the medical unit and down the hall, surrounded by a wall of our security, Sal, and our cousins who have joined us.

Sal looks to Jay, and I don't have to be a mind reader to know what Sal's thinking because the very same thing is going through my mind right now. Who in the family can we trust, cousin after cousin? We thought we had them all, but are there more?

Jay sees us looking and understands our concern. He slows his walk, and I slow mine to match his. "I can assure you, we have no more issues with the family; we've made certain of that, Giovanni.

We'll talk," Jay says, picking up the pace when Sasha turns from her chair to look at him.

When we reach The Larussio tower, Jay swipes his fingerprint over the private elevator's electronic security plate, and the elevator doors close. It stops at the floor right below the penthouse suite, and Serena leans over and hugs Sasha. "We'll talk tomorrow. I'm so glad you are okay," she says, and Sasha hugs her hard.

"Take care of her," I say to Jay as he wheels Sasha out of the elevator and into their suite. The elevator rises to our penthouse, which has now been completely aired and cleared of all the toxins.

I lift Serena from the wheelchair, carry her to our bedroom, and settle her into bed. "I'm so damn sorry this happened. Will you ever be able to get past it?"

She grasps my face, one hand on each of my cheeks, and pulls me closer. "I've always loved your dominance, but when I first learned that you had a tracker on me, I absolutely deplored the notion. After today, I wouldn't have it any other way. You saved my life and the life of our child, Giovanni, because of the control you and the family wield. I love you so much, Giovanni," Serena says.

Epilogue

(4 weeks later)

The Larussio Resort and chapel is all that I could have ever imagined it to be, a vision created in accordance with Carlos Larussio's dream. Always a staunch Catholic, but one even more devout after his brush with death, he wanted the vacationing public to have a place to worship. It was his daughter, though, Katarina Meilers-Larussio-Prestian, who took his vision to a higher level and created not only a place of routine worship, but six different chapels where themed wedding events could be held in accordance with a couple's wildest dreams or fantasies.

My bride walks down the aisle toward me in a long white gown fashioned by one of the most famous men in the world, ordered in Paris just for the occasion. She is surrounded not only by our family and her very close friends, but by all of her friends this time. All flown to Vegas to witness the wedding in The Larussio chapel by our family priest.

When her brother guides her to stand by me this time, there is a genuine smile on his face, unlike the first time. I catch her glimpse over the audience, and the misting of her eyes as she sees her brother's wives and children, her close friends, and many of her previous coworkers sitting in the pews to witness our marriage.

Nonna blows a kiss. She is again sitting by my great-uncle, but this time his arm is around the back of her chair, ensuring her protection and care, as he has done since the first time we married. The wedding is one of the largest the city of Vegas has ever seen and the very first to happen in The Larussio Resort chapel. As I look at Carlos, I see the shine of emotion in his eyes as he holds the hand of his wife sitting next to him.

Chase is holding one of their newborn twins, and his father is holding the other, just barely two weeks old to the day. One boy born approximately three minutes before his baby sister. Katarina's parents are sitting next to Chase, with Brian Carrington and Jenny and Gaby at their side. Carlos could not look any prouder of his great-nephew and his new bride. Jay and Sasha, Matt and Marenah, and the rest of the security team are dispersed throughout the chapel, all invited as guests but ever diligent in their efforts to safeguard the family. Sal and Katarina are standing as best man and maid of honor, a few feet away from us.

When the priest pronounces us husband and wife and I take Serena into my arms, all the weight of the world—the family needs coming first, the need to protect everyone else first and foremost—ceases to exist. While we have not announced it publicly in our circles, I have discussed it with Great-Uncle and have asked Salvatore to take over as Don when he passes. The life of the crime family has never fully been for me, but I have done my best to ensure that the traditions I do believe in were safeguarded while following my own destiny, and will continue to work with Salvatore to ensure the legitimate sides of the family's best interests are managed well into the future.

I crush Serena to me, capturing her lips with my own, before walking down the long aisle past family, friends, and newscasters who are broadcasting our wedding to the entire world. We spend the next hour with photographers, first alone, and then with our wedding party and close family and friends. When the newscasters are allowed into the hall, I provide them with a brief interview, with Serena tucked closely to my side.

The bride-and-groom dance is announced, and I take Serena

into my arms, swaying her softly to the music, and whisper into her ear. "Now all the world knows you are mine, tesoro!" I say, caressing the soft shell of her ear with my lips.

She shivers, and my body responds to her the way it always does, hardening against her softness. I lower my hand to her low back, pressing her against me even firmer, feeling her belly, slightly rounded with our child, pressed against my body. "Mine, always," I whisper as she nuzzles deeper into my chest.

The father-daughter dance commences, and although we discussed this and she knew it could be left out, that instead we could create the wedding dances of our choice, she opted to share this dance with Great-Uncle. I can't make out what he is saying as he spins my wife across the dance floor, but I see the emotion in his eyes, and her own moisten in response.

I inhale deeply. It has been a long road bringing our two families together. At long last, the trust that Serena and I have for each other has spilled to all of our family. I am contemplating this when Salvatore approaches, clapping me on the back.

"Congratulations, cousin. You are beyond blessed," Salvatore says, watching as our great-uncle swirls Serena in his arms to a popular ballad.

"There was a time I would have told you that you were crazy if blessed meant settling for one woman, but Serena has changed all that. Somehow, I knew it from the very first time I held her in my arms. She was destined to be mine," I say, letting my mind wander to the day we met.

He nods. "You will protect her and my godchild and manage all our world resorts and other investments, and I will protect our other family interests."

I smile at him, confident in my decision to turn reign of the Larussio family and those activities over to Salvatore. I follow his gaze as he turns toward the woman in scrubs who has just walked through the door. Katarina and Serena's physician. The one who took care of both Serena and Sasha the night they were taken and lives in one of the penthouses at the resort.

"Guess who just walked in," I say, but I needn't have bothered.

Salvatore's intense eyes haven't missed a move she's made since she walked through that door.

"Excuse me," Salvatore says, stalking toward the pretty, petite blonde with her signature ponytail and crumpled red-and-white Larussio scrubs, who is currently accepting a piece of our wedding cake from a gentleman who seems all too eager to please.

I turn back to Great-Uncle, who is leading Serena off the dance floor and toward me. "I couldn't be happier for the two of you and our family. Now, dance with your wife," Great-Uncle says, leaving us as he weaves his way into the crowd until he comes to stand by Nonna's wheelchair and her grandsons and their families who are surrounding her. Serena's entire family have accepted the Larussios, and that's something I never thought I would live to see.

Katarina and Chase congratulate us, each holding one of the twins and looking so in love and elated over their children. Don Prestian, Chase's father and his new wife, Emily, make their way over to us, along with Carlos and Karissa, Katarina's parents. The men both extend a hand, one, then another, before pulling Serena in for a congratulatory embrace.

After all the years, all the discord, and everything else in between, the family has come full circle and created a new and more diverse family. One in which all of the family factions will now work as one, coming together for the greater good, not only locally but even better, the Larussio family shall reign globally with Salvatore Larussio at its helm.

I pull Serena into my arms and push a strand of her long, dark hair back from her face. She is still the most beautiful woman I have ever seen, and now she is my wife, swollen with our child, and the fear of our enemies ever causing her harm has been put to rest. "I love you, tesoro. You have made me the happiest man in the world. You are mine."

Her eyes shine with emotion as she sinks into me. "Always, Giovanni, always, my love."

Download a free copy of my exclusive story, "A Promise" to receive updates, sneak peeks and fun and games through my newsletter.

A ruthless mafia boss with a score to settle. A sassy heroine who's not getting away. Will any chance at love survive the aftermath? Read the explosive new Boss's Vendetta **next.**

Thank you

Thank you for reading RISE the first in the Brutal Kings series. Reviews help other readers connect to books they may love. Would you be willing to help your fellow readers learn what you love about Giovanni and Serena? If so, please leave a review.

Acknowledgments

Wayne, my husband, thank you for always believing in me, supporting my passions, and helping me make my impossible dream come true.

My parents and family have been a steady reminder that you can achieve your goals with determination, hard work, and commitment. Thank you!

Karla, my dear friend, who read the first book first and encouraged me to keep going, and who recommended getting other beta readers, because "You can only read a book for the first time once." Thank you for your unconditional support through all the insanity!

A special thank you to all the people who diligently bring all the aspects of these novels together. It takes an army, and I may be a bit biased, but this team is fantastic!

Debbie, my amazing street team, and all the groups, bloggers, and book lovers who spread the word about these stories, thank you!

Via's House of Vixens, is a "private" Facebook group for readers and fans to connect. If you would like to be part of this group, request to join for loads of fun!

I hope you continue reading Salvatore Larussio's story in Boss's Vendetta to find out just how delicious, a ruthless mob boss can be.

About Via Mari

Contemporary romantic suspense author Via Mari likes to keep her readers on the edge, fanning themselves as the action unfolds and the heat rises. Her books, featuring the most handsome, intense males, exemplify extreme romance, with powerful men who will stop at nothing to protect the women they love.

Via was raised in both the United States and United Kingdom. Since childhood, she has enjoyed reading books that carry you away. In fact, you can still find her in the early hours of the morning, curled up in an overstuffed chair by a crackling wood fire, reading a page-turning novel, especially during the harsh winters of the Midwestern United States.

When not writing, Via spends her days with her husband. She enjoys gardening, shopping at the local farmers market, and walking in town or around a big city. And she loves traveling to research her next novel.

She also loves interacting with her readers, so feel free to connect with her on the following social media sites! If you want to stay updated on the latest releases and claim a copy of an exclusive story, **sign up for her newsletter.**